MACKEN?

SHADOW REALM SEQUEL

JODY BRADY

Bradyrealms

Copyright © 2020 by Jody Brady. All Rights Reserved

All rights reserved. No part of this book may be reproduced in any form or by any electronic or mechanical means including information storage and retrieval systems without permission in writing from the author except in the case of brief quotations embodied in critical articles and reviews.

This book is a work of fiction. Names, characters, places and incidents are a product of the author's imagination. Any resemblance to actual persons, living or dead is entirely coincidental.

Cover pictures taken from public domain at www.unsplash.com

Printed in the United States of America

First printing December, 2020

Bradyrealms

The Justice Project

Millers Creek, NC

ISBN 9798579819505

If you have read the book, Shadow Realm, and I hope you did, then you only received the partial truth. If you have not read the Shadow Realm, then that's okay, you can still read this account of what has transpired and most likely will understand all, but the first account will help gain all that I wish to share. The tales are my journey, a journey that crosses time and space written as I experienced it, in an order that will seem lost and chaotic at times. I could go right to the end and expose the entire truth that is evident from the very beginning, but what would be the fun of that. The Shadow Realm is only a part of the total, the rest randomly reveals itself that at times makes entirely no sense at all, but in reality includes all that there ever was and ever will be.

The Shadow Realm

PRELUDE *(Long Before)*

  I was alone. I am everything, have always been everything, but I was still lonely for real companionship, true love. I am love in its purest form, yet for love to be fully complete, I needed someone to bestow my love upon.

  I have always spoken things into existence. I think of something that is a part of me, and then I speak, and upon the spoken words, my imagination comes alive, and I have created something new and fresh that is a representation of who I am.

  But I still was lonely in all that I created.

  Time does not exist in my world because I am eternal. I have always been. I will always be.

I AM.

  There is darkness all around, forever darkness, pureness, quiet, myself, eternity. I was conscious of the fact that I was alone in the dark, itself a part of me, a representation of who I am. All creativity rolled up in the darkness before time existed.

  And then the angels were with me as I spoke them into existence, but this was in eternity past before time as you know it existed. But I still felt lonely; my pure love was not complete because, in all that existed before, there was nothing created indeed in the likeness of myself, even though everything was a representation of a part of me.

  I loved the angels, but they are not in all fullness a total representation of who I am.

  I then spoke light into existences and time flowed forth with the light, and there was a beginning as the light of myself exploded outward.

  With my hands, I created humanity you know. Everything else I spoke into existence. But humanity is my highest creation, so speaking the word was not enough.

  I stood on the very edge of the ocean, the waves rushing forward and then receding, held in check by the constraints that I had placed. I reached deep beneath the sands to pull from the earth the pureness of the soil, and from the clay, I formed with all the creativity and love that was within me, I molded humanity in my likeness.

  The angelic host watched from the ocean, from the highest mountain. They fluttered around me, just beyond my reach, waiting in great expectancy, playfully struggling to see what I was creating. They whispered amongst themselves like the children they were. I smiled to myself as I molded humanity, my presence hiding humankind from their inquisitive eyes.

  The ocean waves crashed around me; the wind blew ever so slightly as I meticulously formed humanity, the face, arms, legs, fingers, hair. I placed the organs, the heart that would hold my blood already shed before. I modeled the intricate DNA that comes directly from my own.

Angels fluttered close. I waved them off and then placed humanity in the garden that I had already created.

Humanity stood there before me, not yet alive, only flesh. The angels were perplexed. Everything else that I had created immediately came to life upon my spoken word, but humanity just stood there before me, perfect in creation, beautiful above all else, yet not alive.

What is this? The angels asked. What have you done? I did not answer them.

I only smiled and stood back against the ocean, the water pulling back away from my presence. The birds gathered overhead; the fish peered above the water; the animals watched from the forests. All my creation knew that something marvelous was about to happen. All the creation waited expectantly. The animals spoke among themselves according to their kind, but nothing approached me to ask me directly what I was about to do. Like the angels, I would not have answered.

I let them continue to wonder.

I continued to stand and look down at humanity as humankind stood before me, still asleep, no life within.

All creation suddenly gasped as I reached down to take the man I had created in my hands, placed my mouth over his and breathed my Spirit, my Life, all that I am, into his lungs.

And your eyes immediately opened in awe and wonder in your mother's womb where I created you individually.

Humanity's first breath was deep and long. My Spirit rushed through the body, and blood flowed, the heartbeat, DNA fluttered to life.

In the womb, you awoke with the first sight being my eyes looking into yours. There was no fear, no confusion, and no hesitancy. Only a full realization that you were created to be just like me.

I knew in the beginning that humanity would betray me, but in a way that only I can understand the blood had already been shed. I knew that humanity would come back to me with a fresh understanding of who I am, who you are that only life's journey can produce.

So, although I felt the pain of betrayal, it did not bother me too much. Yes, I was saddened by the knowledge that humanity would reject me, and my heart lay broken. But the understanding that humankind would return covered my pain with joy.

The angels thought that humanity would ask me questions. They wished to but did not. They fluttered closer to take a look, awed by the beauty *and the knowledge that the spark of life that only I possess was now alive within humanity. I brushed them gently away.*

I took a step closer to you when you accepted my love and placed you back in the garden that I had first created.

A large rock jutted out from among the lush flowers in the garden among the shade of the towering oak trees nearby. I set upon it watching humanity's first reaction to the garden I had created. I remember it as if it were just yesterday, although I guess that it was just a flicker of time ago in fact. The afternoon was hot, the sun bearing down in newness of life.

The angels had left humanity's garden to take care of the rest of my creation because I only wanted to be with you. In the womb when I first created you, in your journey when you rejected me, now in the garden where you are meant to be as a new creation.

You tried to climb up the rock to reach me when you awoke again to my presence but could not in your strength. I reached down and took your hand and pulled you gently up to where I sat. And we sat together side by side watching the first sunrise of your new life.

Humanity was as a newborn baby when I first placed him in the garden. Everything humanity felt, tasted, smelled, heard, saw was new and fresh and beautiful.

The wonder in your eyes when you awoke to my presence and I placed you back in the garden again made it all worthwhile.

May your whole spirit, soul and body be kept blameless at the coming of our Lord, Jesus Christ. I Thessalonians, 5:23(NIV)

THE PHYSICAL REALITY

The young girl had traveled for weeks through the forest since the night she was attacked, and left for dead, her torment overwhelming as the drugs that her body depended on for life, were no longer in her. She had hidden in caves or the deep forest, once in an abandoned barn. The hallucinations that haunted her mind seemed to be everywhere.

She was starving. The whole world seemed to be one constant nightmare, brought on by the drugs she had taken and then by the sickness caused as they had left her system craving more and causing her to see things that could not be true, or could they? She could no longer tell the difference.

And then she came upon the rock house.

The rock house stood in a small meadow beneath several ancient oaks whose limbs shaded the structure from the sun. Lingering snow lay among the shaded areas. The frigid, morning air caused the girl to shiver even though she wore both sets of clothes she had, plus the wool overcoat. She desperately needed food.

Smoke flowed upward from the chimney. Behind the house, a barn and chicken coup stood. Several chickens scratched among the grass in front of the house. Where there were chickens, there were eggs, she thought to herself. If she sneaked around the back of the barn, she could get to the coup and take a few of the eggs.

She ran along the tree line to the back of the house and darted quickly across the yard to the end of the barn. Peering through the cracks between the wall planks, she saw a milk cow eating from hay that had recently been placed in the stall. She backed quickly away from the crack when she saw an older woman tossing hay in the stall.

"Now there you go Emily. Good hay for you ole girl."

The woman patted the appreciative cow and picked up a bucket of milk that still steamed in the morning air. The girl looked back into the barn, yearning for the fresh milk. She edged her way to the corner of the barn and looked around the structure in time to see the woman enter the house through the back door. The chicken coup was only ten feet away. She waited until the door closed and then she started to cross the yard to the fence when suddenly the door opened, and the woman walked back out into the yard. The girl ducked back to the barn and watched as the woman opened a small door next to the coup and emerged a minute later with a bucket of grains. She threw the corn across the ground in front of the chicken coup, and a dozen hens scampered quickly over to feast on the breakfast. She then entered the coup and filled her small basket with a dozen or so large brown eggs and walked back into the house.

The girl watched in vain as the eggs left her sight. She almost cried as she slumped down to the ground next to the barn. The last weeks had been a blur of death and horror. If she did not eat soon, she would die. She had to get into that house and get food, but how?

She heard the door open and peered around the barn again. The woman walked back toward the chicken coup, but this time she carried freshly baked bread. She stopped halfway between the house and barn and stood, holding out the food and looking toward the sky, turning her head as if she were listening. She took another step and turned to face the barn. There was something strange about the way she looked at the barn.

"Child, I know you are nearby. Don't be afraid. You are starving. I have food. Please, child, I can help you."

The girl stood up. She smelled the bread and her stomach pain intensified with anticipation. How had the woman known that she hid by the barn?

"Please child. I won't hurt you. I can help, but you must hurry. I can only protect you if you are with me."

The girl stepped cautiously away from the wall. She had to eat something.

The woman turned to face her, "Please come closer child so that I can see you."

The girl was only ten feet away from the woman who stared straight into her. She was blind, the girl thought.

Nicole stepped closer.

"There you are child. On my, you look a sight. Please take this bread. I was going to fry eggs and ham for breakfast."

The girl reached out and took the bread. It was warm and covered in butter. She lustfully ate the bread, finishing the small loaf in a couple of bites.

The woman laughed, "Oh my child, you are hungry. Please come in. I have plenty to eat and a warm fire."

The woman turned and walked back to the house, the girl following behind her.

The kitchen was small, just large enough for a small table with four chairs, a bar and cabinets down one side with a sink and wood stove. There were other appliances including a modern stove and refrigerator

"Please sit child. I will feed you and then you can take a warm bath."

The woman opened the door to the refrigerator and took out a pitcher, pouring the contents into a glass cup. The girl had only seen cups such as this one at the mayor's house at home. It looked like crystal. The woman stopped with the glass looking toward the girl but appeared not to see her. She walked closer, "There you are," she placed the cup on the table.

"How about ham and eggs, child," she smiled.

The girl shook her head. She was still starving. She could not say anything. How could such a peaceful place be in the middle of the horrors that surrounded it?

The woman opened the door again and brought out the ham and several eggs. She turned the knobs and to the girl's surprise, a blue flame shot upward from the top of the appliance. It was only a few minutes longer, and the woman sat a plate in front of her and then sat across from her with a plate of her own.

She took a sip of the cold drink. It was fresh orange juice. She immediately gulped it down and then began to eat the food. The woman watched as she finished the plate, not saying a word.

When the girl finished, the woman poured her another glass of the juice.

She took another drink, then was suddenly embarrassed.

"Thank you," she stammered. "It has been over a week since I have eaten anything more than a bit of bread."

The woman smiled, "What is your name child?" she asked.

The girl told her.

"I am Nicole," the woman replied, a wide smile on her aged face. She had blue eyes that seem to glaze over a bit, blond hair and a tanned face, "Where have you come from, child?"

The girl instantly trusted the woman, reminding her of a long-ago grandma that had shown her love before she had been taken away.

"I am from beyond the forest," was all the girl could think to say. It was a partial truth, but what else could she tell the woman. She had been living in a tent city, far from the town where she had grown up, where her life had been destroyed by evil men who used her, who sold her body to whoever, who filled her with drugs and then who had discarded her.

She began to shake, staring out the window, fear building. The hallucinations could come suddenly, tearing all reality from what was left of her mind.

"No worries child. You're safe here." Nicole placed her hand over the girl's.

The hand was warm, the skin soft and wrinkled with age.

The girl glanced nervously out the kitchen window to the black forested tree line on the horizon. Far off, against the mountain, a thin trail of black smoke drifted upward and then just as quickly disappeared. The black forest changed to a dark green as the tree line wavered.

She rubbed her eyes and looked again. The green trees were gone, only a burned-out wasteland remained as far as she could see. Horses galloped through the smoke toward the house! Death!

She stood up and screamed. She had to run!

"What is it, child?" Nicole cried, grabbing the girl's arm as she pulled away, knocking the dishes across the floor.

"Nicole, we have to run. They will kill us all!"

The girl screamed and turned, but Nicole held her with surprisingly strong arms.

"No child, there is nothing there. You are safe here,"

The girl struggled against Nicole.

"Look child! There is no one coming. You are safe child."

Nicole pointed toward the forest, and the girl froze, staring out the window. She saw the meadow, barn, and chicken coup. Cattle and sheep grazed near the tree line. There was no smoke, no horseman. Only the dark green of the pine forest against the horizon. What was going on?

"But they were there. They were coming for me," the girl gasped. She was losing her mind in this place.

Nicole pulled her tighter against her in a lovingly embrace, "Child. Nothing can hurt you in this place."

The girl buried her head against the older woman's breast. She suddenly did feel safe, totally safe, a feeling that she had not felt since a child.

Nicole looked intently at the girl she held. Her sight was just strong enough to see the blackened wasteland, the mad horseman, the smoke. But they were in a realm that could not affect her in this place, ever present, but just across the veil.

Later that night, both women sat in the living room. The girl lay by a fireplace under a blanket as the wind blew strongly outside the glass window. Nicole read from a large, leather bound book by the light from a small lamp that glowed a bright white light. The girl wanted to ask her hostess more about the place. Why she felt so safe? Why the hallucinations seem to have left her? Why for the first time in a long time did she feel at total peace? But the weariness of her last few weeks of ordeal pulled at her, and she fell asleep by the fire, the warmth against her face soothing.

Nicole glanced up at the child as she slept, her face peaceful in the fire's light. Nicole did not understand what had happened to cause the girl to suddenly appear in her yard by the barn. She had been milking the cow when she suddenly saw a vision of a great fire, horsemen riding across a ravaged countryside that wavered in a mist just past her pastureland. And then a girl had appeared out of the fog, running up to the barn.

She saw the child again, as she fed the chickens, appear and re-appear and she knew that somehow the girl was real flesh and blood and desperately needed a place of warmth and safety. Just like all the girls that she had saved those many years ago as she and her husband worked to expose the sex trade and abuse of young girls. Her husband was dead now, having gone on to his reward for over 80 years of ministry. That had been over a year ago, she thought, which made her. She had to think a minute. Oh my, she thought, I am 101 years old now.

She looked lovingly at the pictures of her and Tom that sat on the end table next to her. She still felt his presence. She also felt the presence of her God, who told her what she must do to help the girl. Nicole placed the bible and another book by the girl. The book had been written by her husband after he had once almost died on the fire in Wyoming. She thought of that time. What a strange story he had told her of his experiences. That had been the beginning of a whole new chapter in their lives. It was a time when the veil between realms had opened to them, a time when the present order of things had drastically changed.

The girl awoke suddenly in the night. She silently watched as Nicole placed two books on the table next to her and pulled the blanket up to her neck. No one had done that to her since she had been a small child, she thought. She waited until the elderly woman left the room and then she turned the lamp back on and looked at the books.

The first one was the Bible, which was what Nicole had been reading earlier. She did not wish to read that book, she thought. The bible brought back bad memories of a father who had abused her as a child, who had been a minister but treated her terribly. He had used the words in that book for his gain. He had used the words in that book to condemn her, even though she was a child. He had used the words in that book to justify his abusive actions. She would not read that book, she thought. But the second one intrigued her.

The book was tiny, only thirty pages in length. On the cover was a simple title which read "The Garden, by Tom Mackenzie."

She began to read from the first page. She would have never believed at the time that reading that one book would change her life forever.

CHAPTER ONE

I, Jonathan, stood at the abyss that is my past. Where does the trail lead? I ask myself. Malak had warned me to beware that I did not stray from the path while being drawn toward the distant shore, where the only real love that I had ever known was rumored to be a captive.

Great victories had been gained. The portal across the river to safety was strong now, guarded by warriors both human and Bene Elohim, but much was still to be done for the ancient curse to be destroyed forever. I was the Apostolic Or, the Light Giver. I knew that now. The sacrifice of those before me had taught me that. I never wished to betray their trust in me, even though I felt that I had to go.

I figured that Malak would have stopped me. He could have quickly forced me back with the strength of arms, but that was not the Bene Elohim's way. They guided humans, fought for us, assisted us in time of need, but they never interfered in our right to choose our path, even if that path could lead to destruction.

I stood by my horse at the entrance to the monuments of life, a broken wall of granite barring my way. The last time I had been here, I had been running for my life, a dying fugitive trusting me for her salvation, two warriors of Kratos hunting us in the night. Now I was alone. Heather and Peter stood guard at the gates of Soteria, leading a growing army of newly released fugitives. How their love for each other had grown this past year.

With great sadness, I thought of Patrick, who had given his life so that I would gain my freedom. Had I betrayed him as well with my decision? No, I would not do that. I was still the Apostolic Or. I held the key to destroy the Shadow Realm once and for all, but even after a year, I still did not truly understand what that key was.

Word had come to us that Lillian was taken a prisoner, that she was held captive and only I had the power to free her. My friends understood my need to go and save her. I had always wished to go before, but the time had not been right. Even now it was a chance, but a chance that I was willing to take. I had broken the power of Krino over the land of the fugitives. Our army was growing each day as refugees fled to the river crossing to gain their freedom. I could not wait any longer. I had to save the girl that I loved, and so I had left.

Now I could no longer see the way through the monuments. It was all just a vast expanse of destruction, failures, disobedience, mistrust, and pride. But I now knew that I had to get it right finally. I would have to trust the Light that was my freedom entirely.

I could not see and then suddenly there appeared shafts of pure, white light escaping through slits in several large, wooden doors that dropped out of the darkness.

Which way to go? Open which door? I did not even dare to walk through the door that Malak had told me to follow, that I knew now was the right way to go. How could I go through one of those that stood before me now? But I could not go back. The walls were surrounding me now, and I had no way back out of the monuments of life. The trail behind had crumbled away as I passed by, leaving only open space and total blackness that revealed even darker shadows that roll like the ocean waves on a calm day.

My future depends on my decision. My life, Lillian's life, Soteria itself, depends on my steps. Which door?

And then I knew for a certainty that could only come from the Light itself that glowed within me, that it did not matter which one I chose. They all led me toward the pure light shining through the slits. The key is not necessarily which door to open that is placed before me by the Light. The key is to break through one of them until I am totally immersed in the Light behind the door and entirely trust the One that was slain before, the fourth man in the Light, the Light itself. Otherwise, I would remain in the dark, next to the abyss, which is my past.

I drew the broadsword given to me by Patrick and mounted my horse, who snorted with anticipation, stomping his feet and pushing forward. I chose the center door, and the Light within me exploded outward.

CHAPTER TWO

The Light vanished from around me, and I stood on a sandy shore washed in the full moon's light. Where was my horse? I did not understand what had happened to me as I passed through the monuments. Lillian was alive! I could not tell what was happening to her, but I knew where she was.

Something had happened to me the night I had left Lillian by the river. It was as if a part of me was torn away. I did not feel the emptiness at the time, because all was so new. The Light was a part of me. My chains had been destroyed, and for the first time in my life, I was free. I had been the Apostolos Or, the Light Giver, the first in the land of the fugitives in my lifetime to find the Light and unlock its power.

Patrick, Peter, Heather and I had escaped to the river and had defeated Archon Krino at the river crossing which had broken his control over all the land of the fugitives. I had been embraced by the Soterians who lived in the village across the river. Under the guidance of the Bene Elohim, Malak and Nasar, we had gathered a growing army of fugitives who crossed the river each day to embrace the Light.

But when news had come that Lillian was being held captive by Archon Planos, the emptiness within me grew. Something began to change within me. Something lay just out of reach, a distant memory of wholeness, of something lost. I had asked about these things to Malak, but he had told me that only I could work to understand the mystery. That this journey, I would have to take alone. And so here I was, standing in an unknown realm on a sandy shore, in the middle of the night. And then I looked across the beach and saw the wall and a gate.

The massive wooden gate loomed over me, the spiked metal hinges bleeding orange from ancient rust caused by the ever-present salty spray of the ocean. I could smell the ocean, feel the sting in the salt air, hear the crashing waves, but could not see the water. The wall blocked my way, stretching along the sandy beach out of sight in both directions into the darkness of the night. A full moon washed the dunes behind me in a pale glow, the breeze caressing the scattered clumps of grass that waved back and forth.

    I stood before the gate perplexed at what I should do and then walked tentatively up to the gate. Chains, the links larger than a man's hand, shackled the two doors together, secured with a single lock. I pulled at the chains, but they were too heavy, and I was unable to move them. The lock was too heavy as well. There appeared to be no place else to go, nothing more than I could do.

    I had never seen the ocean. The elders had told me that the sea spread as far as the eye could see off to the place where the sun retreated at the end of each day. I could not fathom anything that would compare with such a sight, and now I stood before the wall, the vast ocean pressing against the other side. The door moaned eerily in the night, the great beams forever fighting the tremendous weight of the wall of water that continually pushed to break through.

    There were places along the wall where the sand was wet as the water seeped under. Small rivulets of glistening water ran down both sides of the gate. To my surprise, the water tasted salty. I pressed my gloved hands against the cold iron and immediately felt a deep stirring from deep within the hinges. I pulled off my gloves and again rubbed both hands down the iron. The rust was wet from the water and turned my hands dark. I could now only hear water running somewhere, the sound of the crashing waves suddenly gone. I felt constant pressure from the other side of the gate as it cracked and buckled as if in turmoil, straining with all its strength to keep whatever was bound up on the other side from crushing it. The constant moaning cast a melancholy shadow. What a shame it was that whatever was caged on the other side could not be free, I thought.

    The wind stirred even more than before and then suddenly blew hard for just a moment, spraying me with cold salty water, pelting my face with fine sand. A whisper called forth from somewhere in the darkness, faint and haunting, blowing in with the wind, and I stepped back from the gate, and the whisper ceased. What had it said? Where had it come from?

    I looked apprehensively around, holding the hilt of my knife at my waist with one hand while reaching out with a shaking hand to touch the gate again. I grabbed the giant chains, and yet the whispers called out from somewhere on the other side. The whispers grew stronger than before even as the wind blew stronger. Somewhere far off in the darkness, past the great wall, thunder rumbled, and the sky flashed brightly for a split second among towering clouds. A storm was approaching.

I leaned closer to the gate. Drawn by the growing whispers from the other side, I placed my ear against the rough beams, holding the chains with both hands. What were the strange voices saying? It was as if thousands of people were all continually whispering, their individual voices intermingling, yet all were saying the same thing.

Suddenly the sun blinded me. Crashing over my head was a wall of seething, churning, blue-green water, curling up and over me in one momentous wave of pure power and raw beauty. Fearful in its power, the surge gained height and strength, the white frosted lip extending over my head, blocking the sun and causing a multicolored rainbow to wash over me. Terrified, I turned to flee the crashing water, deafening now and full of uncontrolled power so great that it could tear away the shoreline, break over the mountains and forever engulf the land under its blue-green cover. Like it had once been long ago in the beginning.

The whispers were now one great terrifying scream, "Release me!"

I turned away from the gate, falling face down in the sand fully expecting the wave to crash down over me, but it disappeared just as suddenly as it had appeared. I breathed deep, my heart racing with continued fear and I turned over, leaning back on my elbows to gaze upward into the night and towering walls.

"Quite a fright, wasn't it?" a voice spoke from high above the gate.

I backed up quickly and stood.

I searched the shadows for the origin of the voice but saw no one. A man jumped down from a ladder by the gate. He dusted the sand from his loose-fitting trousers and took a step out from the darkness by the wall and into the full moon's pale light.

I pointed my knife at the man, "That will be far enough sir," I demanded.

"Whoa, now sir. I mean you no harm. I was commenting on what you have just seen."

I eyed the man suspiciously. He was a small man with short, cropped, dark hair with a bowl cut over a round face and large eyes.

He wore a loose white shirt tied in the front with puffed sleeves and a wide black belt with dark pants that puffed out over his legs before disappearing under high black boots. A short sword was at his side, and the pearl-handled hilt caught the moon's reflection.

"How did you know what I just saw?" I asked.

"I have seen many react to the gate because of the vision of the power locked behind those doors. I too have seen the vision and heard the whispering voices."

I lowered the knife, but observed the stranger, glancing around to ensure that there were no others nearby. I had always been distrustful of strangers, but for some reason, I did not fear this particular one. Maybe it was because of his outlandish dress and manner. How long had he been watching me? For some reason, what had happened before to bring me to this place, no longer mattered. It was as if that had been a dream and this place was where I had been all along.

"Do you make it a practice of spying on travelers, sir?" I asked.

"No, no lad. But you have seen a great mystery, have you not? It is said that the Bene Elohim's father built the walls himself to keep the great oceans from covering the entire land. If you could have opened the gate, I believe that the vision would have become a reality."

"I have never heard such as this before. I do not know where I am sir, but I have heard tales of the great ocean and that the Bene Elohim ruled over a kingdom beyond the sea.

"It is very rare indeed to see a young man by the wall, alone in this place in the middle of the night."

"Just as strange as seeing a little man jump down from a wall out of the darkness," I responded, observing the man.

The man chuckled and held out his arms, his palms outward.

"I agree sir. Forgive me for my abruptness, but I have witnessed many who have fled after seeing the vision, but you did not but turned to face it."

"I have run enough out of fear. I will not do that any longer."

"Brave words young one, but there is much in this land that is fearful unless you can discern the truth behind it," the man took a step further away from the wall, turning his head slightly as if listening. He began to speak, then stopped himself and suddenly bowed, tipping his feathered hat.

"Please forgive me, sir. My name is Crestos, Keeper of the Wall, a member of the Shore Guards of King Elohim. At your service."

I stood silent for a moment, taken aback by the sudden formality. What place had I found myself?

"My name is Jonathan."

"Where are you from Sir Jonathan?"

"At the moment, I do not know. I was in the Monuments of Life, and suddenly I found myself here, in this place."

"Oh yes, the Monuments of Life. Why were you traveling through that maze? You have to be searching for something, sir. What may that be?"

I thought for a moment before answering the man. I was used to the Light showing me the way, but for some reason, the Light worked differently in this place. The Light was all around me as if it was a part of the landscape itself. I was suddenly confused, uncertain of what I was to say.

For some reason, I did not wish to answer the man, "That is of no concern to you Mr. Crestos."

"Of course, of course. I did not mean to pry. We all seek something in this life," Crestos turned to look up at the wall.

"Like me for instance. I spend days, sometimes weeks walking the wall seeking those who wish to see the grandeur that is the ocean. To see the beauty that King Elohim has created for all to enjoy if they can but see beyond the veil that hides it."

"What do you mean?" I stepped forward, the man's words drawing out from me an inward desire to see through the veil, to see the creation made for my kind.

Crestos continued, "Most people do not see past the initial horror that would be if the walls were not set in place to keep the ocean at bay, but everything in this land is not what it appears to be. Even the light of day can be hidden by the darkness of the night. King Elohim has many treasures that are only found by those that seek the truth. Do you seek truth?"

"I found the Truth, sir. The Light is the Truth, but for some reason, it has led me to this place."

I did not understand what was happening. What realm had I suddenly found myself in? It was as if I had somehow seen myself behind a mirror. Which side was the real world?

As if understanding my confusion, Crestos spoke, "Let me show you what is really behind the wall. I assure you that you will not be disappointed."

I took a step forward with his words. The great wall loomed ominously in the darkness, a pale light glowing behind it.

"I saw a horrid vision of death and destruction before. I felt the gates labored torment as they fight to hold back the water. I heard the screams behind the gate. I do not wish to experience that again."

"You will not. Trust me, sir. I am the Keeper of the Wall. My job is to ensure that the wall continues to hold back the destructive power of the ocean. Yes, the ocean screams to be released, but the wall was set in the beginning to hold it in place. But the wall is only a representation of King Elohim's power. The truth is only found when one stands on top of the wall. Then you can see what the creation looks like."

I hesitated. I did wish to see behind the wall, but could I trust this man?

Crestos smiled at me, holding out his hand, "Come Jonathan. All you have to do is take a step with me, and you will be able to see past this reality to the truth beyond. The real kingdom is just on the other side. But it is your choice and your choice alone. No one can force you to go. I certainly will not.

"Just take one step with me. If you do not feel comfortable with what you see, all you must do is turn away, and you will be back on this side of the wall. I promise. You have traveled far. Don't let it be in vain."

I took a step toward the gate that suddenly vanished in a cloud of silver dust.

It was full daylight, the sun an orange ball of warmth and comfort in a deep blue sky. How could this be?

We both stood on a wide, sandy beach that stretched in both directions beyond the horizon. I gasped in wonderment at the pure beauty of the endless, deep green ocean before me, the white-capped waves caressing the shore in a continuous successive dance with a rhythm orchestrated by the most excellent conductor.

A breeze carried the strong, salty smell of the water as well as fine sand that peppered my face. I breathed in deeply, filling my lungs with the intoxicating aroma. The white caps crashed over into the calmer water beneath us and rolled forward, losing all of their strength as the water swelled up almost to my knees before receding into the depths. Each wave following the last, all of them exhausting their force in a vain attempt to overtake the shore, only to crash in a turmoil of white, frothy, churning water before retreating into the depths, as if something prevented the waves from continuing inland.

"Where did the wall go Crestos?"

"Oh, the wall is still here. The water crashes against it with each wave. But this is the true reality. This is the true creation."

"And you say that King Elohim created this?"

"Yes. the Creator separated the water from the land and then placed the wall to forever keep the oceans in check."

"It is stunning," I remarked, staring out across the endless sea, the wide sandy beach, and the seagulls floating on the wind currents above. How could the King have created all of this?

"What do you truly search for Jonathan?" Crestos suddenly asked.

How could I answer that question? Yes, I was trying to reach Lillian, but there was something more, something I could not grasp, a mystery that the Light seemed to point toward, but did not yet fully reveal. And in this place, the Light worked differently. It was as if it was everything around me, all at one time.

"I truly do not know anymore. And now here, in this place, all seems so strange. Everything seems reversed somehow. What is real and what is not?" I asked.

Crestos smiled. "Yes, this place will do that to a person. There are many layers, Jonathan, but there is only one true kingdom. It was never meant to be this way and one day it will all change, but for now, you must learn to see. But I have something that I think will help you in your quest."

Crestos reached from under his cloak and pulled out a weathered, leather book and handed it to me.

"This is a journal written by someone long ago that will show you the truth behind the veil. And remember the current reality was never meant to be. The true kingdom is out there."

And I suddenly found myself standing among the rocks deep within the maze that was the Monuments of Life, my horse grazing on the grass next to me. I looked at the book Crestos had given me, perplexed at the strange realm I had found myself in. I opened the first page and read a bit of the text written in cursive with black ink.

For sixteen days, I stopped whatever I was doing when I felt God wanted to speak and wrote exactly what I heard the Lord speak to me without reading anything until He told me to stop writing. I then read what I had written and was astonished at what God had spoken to my spirit. The message was a message of true love. Hopefully, it will be to you as well. Mackenzie

And with a violent flash of light, I was no longer in my story, but Lillian's

CHAPTER THREE

Darkness all around, so thick that it was crushing, no sound but the girl's heavy breathing as she lay in the ditch filled with water. Lillian held her head just above the water. She laid perfectly still, her heart pounding loudly within her. Out in the blackness that was a stormy, winter night, someone moved among the towering pines. A twig loudly snapped a few feet away, and she instinctively held her breath. She ran her tongue over her lips, tasting blood and sweat. Her head throbbed. The freezing water pulled at her senses with its seductive caress, numbing her hands and feet and slowly climbing up her legs and arms, her back and shoulders until only her head remained just above its deadly seduction.

She had fallen in the darkness, rolled over a log and slipped into the water, breaking the thin veil of ice. The water gladly swallowed her into its embrace, quickly pulling her life's heat from her body as if it were a living organism that only survived with her warmth. Now she lay freezing to death, but she knew that to move was to die, but not before her pursuers had their way with her. She shuddered inwardly at the thought and continued to suffer in silence

The icy pain was not as severe now, Lillian thought. The cold fingers that had first assaulted her senses with pain now caressed her with a warmer nothingness. She could end it here and now. Just slip her head entirely under the water, allow the veil to close over her and lose herself in the numbness. She immediately shook her head at the thought and again heard movement nearby. Someone crept through the forest.

She glanced up and over the log and saw the torch blazing a hot orange that cast an eerie iridescent light through the otherwise dark forest. Shadows danced among the trees. Two men walked side by side, searching for her. Their great coats and hats, waist-length hair and beards exposed only their faces to the extreme cold. They resembled wild animals more than men, but they were indeed men, savage and brutal, but men.

Lillian wiggled her fingers and toes and was immediately rewarded with hot flashes of icy pain. She knew that she had to get out of the water soon, or she would freeze to death, but she was too afraid of the two men to move. They walked alarmingly close until the torchlight washed ever so slightly over the log and across her face. She held her breath and immersed her head under the water, closing her eyes as she did so.

The two men stood for a few seconds by the log and then turned away. The girl turned her head so she could breathe and watched as the light retreated away from the ditch.

"She is lost, that one," the taller man remarked.

"She will freeze to death in this weather mate. Let's go back. Her body will no doubt feed the wolves."

The tall one switched the torch to his other hand, "It's a shame she slipped away. I was hoping to feed on her body myself."

They both laughed, their voices echoing through the forest. Shadows continued to dance among the trees.

"We have others. Let's get back to camp."

Lillian breathed again, shuttering at the memories of the previous night. The memories were forever etched into her mind, memories of murder and brutality, rape and destruction. The savages had come upon them suddenly out of the dark forest. Their small camp walls were no match for the warriors with their battering rams and catapults, armored chariots and knights on horseback. The fire quickly destroyed the gate, and the black hordes of death had swiftly ridden through the camp, killing all who opposed them.

Lillian had watched from her hiding place with three other young girls her age until darkness. Then under cover of the night, the four girls had slipped through a gap in the wooden palisade and out into the freezing world of snow and ice.

One of the savages had spotted them as they had run across the meadow and moments later the beasts began searching through the forest like wolves for their prey. In the darkness, the four quickly became separated as they ran frantically among the great cathedral of tall pines. Many times, they had walked in the forest together during the day, but they had never been outside of the camp walls at night. Since the Bene Elohim had attacked her clan by the river, her father had withdrawn the clan behind fortified walls near Halom for safety.

What a lie that had been, Lillian thought as she eased herself out of the water and over the log immediately beginning to shiver in the cold night air. She would freeze for sure unless a miracle saved her. Lillian thought again of the four girls' flight for freedom. One by one she had heard the screams of her friends as they had been caught somewhere in the darkness behind her. Three times she heard the screams and howls of lust from the savages and then suddenly she was alone in a black world of death.

The two men with their torch were gone, but there was a small bit of moonlight filtering down through the forest canopy. Lillian tried to stand up on her numb feet, and at first, she could feel nothing and began to panic and then the pain returned as the blood started to flow again. The distant fires from the camp glowed in the darkness. Her home, her family, her innocence all gone in a single day.

What was she to do now? She shook violently then, her body rebelling against the freezing water that hung over her with icy fingers. She looked back through the forest and saw movement among the blueberry bushes, now covered with a light powdering of snow. The snow slipped off from the bushes. She forced her legs to walk slowly toward the movement until she heard a faint whimper of pain. The numbness had left her feet and legs, replaced by the pain of possible frostbite, but Lillian ignored the new sensation and ran quickly to the sound.

Her friend lay naked in the snow, her body glowing a pale white in the moon's caress, her back smeared in mud and blood. Lillian dropped down beside her, but the girl was already dead. When the savages had finished with her, they had cut her throat, the girl's life-giving blood pouring out over the ground, turning the snow dark.

Lillian looked around her and then back to the burning encampment. She thought that she heard screaming far off in the distance. She could not go back, could never trust the city walls again. The gates had not withstood the enemy, and now her family was dead, and her best friend lay naked and violated beneath her. She began to shutter again as she cried, a gut retching cry from deep within her soul, a soul that would forever be wounded by what she had experienced this past day and night. Her clothes were freezing against her now, and she suddenly stopped crying. She had to somehow get to a fire, but how? Lillian gently laid her friend's head down and stood up, turning to the fire.

The glow called to her with its promise of warmth, but she knew that she dared not go to it. Certain death or slavery awaited her there. No, she would rather freeze to death in the dark as a free woman than to go back to the camp with its lies and the black horde. She glanced back down to where her friend lay and saw the peace across her face in death. And then she spotted the pile of clothes nearby, clothes that the men had torn from the girl.

Lillian quickly gathered them up. They were torn a bit, but she could wear them, and most importantly, they were dry. She pulled her wet shirt off and placed the dry one over her. It fit just fine. The trousers and black boots fit just as well. Her friend had also worn a heavy woolen overcoat that went down past her knees. Lillian remembered the day that the girl's father had given the coat to her. She had been jealous the first time she had seen the jacket, wishing that she could have one as well. She dismissed the memory and tied her new pants tightly around her thin waist with her rope belt and gathered up her clothes, tying them in a bundle.

Lillian knelt and kissed her friend on the cheek in farewell and turned away from the fire's glow. She had no idea where she would go but knew that she would never return to her childhood home. Her family had been happy and free until the night the Bene Elohim had raided their camp, the night that Jonathan had betrayed her and brought the Light and its warriors to her family. She had trusted him. She had loved him, but he had betrayed them all.

The council had promised to assist them, but once in Halom, they had been attacked again, this time by warriors of a strange beastly race of men that no one had ever seen before. Somewhere out there in the darkness, the truth lay hidden, and she swore that she would find it. Jonathan had brought the Light among them, and now her family lay dead in the snow. He had said that the Light would free her of her chains of death, but she had no chains around her. The nomads were already free.

Jonathan had betrayed her, and he was somewhere out there across the river, and she swore by the blood of her family that she would find him and expose the Bene Elohim for what they were. She would ask him why he had left them to die. She would make him pay for betraying her. But first, she had to find him.

CHAPTER FOUR

Zanah sat upon her warhorse high up among the craggy mountains overlooking the lower hills of Halom and the burning encampment. The air was brutally cold, the wind blowing her long hair across her face, momentarily covering her eyes. She pulled the unruly locks back and tucked them into her headband as she watched below. The horse stomped impatiently, his nostrils flaring and blowing hot breath across his face, his red eyes casting pale light across the shadows of the night. He was a warhorse of the Sahat. Behind her, several of her guard sat motionless upon their horses.

Once roaming the Plains of Sin from Archon Krino's training camps in search of chained fugitives, the dreaded Sahat warriors had mysteriously disappeared with the banishment of their master at the hands of the Apostolic Or. Now that portion of the Shadow Realm that had been under Archon Krino's control was in anarchy with no rule of law. The chained fugitives had disappeared from the eastern Plains of Apistia and the great forest entirely to the great city Hedone where Archon Sarkinos ruled only within his city walls. The human knights of Kratos were leaderless at present, having fortified their great citadel to await the master's orders. Archon Athemitos, taking advantage of the void created by the absence of Krino, had spread out from his power base at Soma and now raided at will wherever it pleased him.

Only Archon Planos held his original territory. In fact, in the chaos after the order of law under Krino had been broken, Archon Planos' realm had grown stronger, which was his plan all along. Deception was truly a powerful force, and Zanah had taken great advantage of the raid by her soldiers masquerading as Bene Elohim on Connelly's nomad band as they had camped by the river. All of the nomads totally under Archon Planos' control now believed that the Light that had appeared in the hands of the young fugitive was evil and threatened their existence.

But scouts had reported back to the Master that the Light was growing stronger in the wild lands of the great forest after

Krino had been defeated. A new plan had been devised to destroy it by destroying the fugitive, Zanah could not think of him as anything else but a fugitive, who had used the Light's mysterious power to destroy Krino.

She watched emotionless as nomads were dispatched by the horde warriors of Archon Athemitos who had dared to raid across the river into the realm of Archon Planos. Across the great meadows of Halom, lay the walled Council village and nomad encampments under the cliffs of the Crystalline Mountains that hid the power base and home of Planos and Zanah. Standing high on the battlements, Planos stood watching the same scene.

Zanah could not see her counterpart but could feel his presence.

"Why do we stand and watch as the mongrel Athemitos kills our subjects?" Zanah asked the night sky.

She had no care for the nomads herself; she only cared that she would not be the one who could do the killing in her own time, her pleasure.

"You are displeased by my decision to allow the raid?" she heard Planos' answer flow back to her on the cold wind.

"You knew he was coming?" Zanah questioned.

"Oh, my dear, beautiful enchantress. You are not the only one who can play with the minds of our fellow Archons. Now take your warriors, go down and drive out the raiders and make sure to save the girl Lillian who is hiding by the river. Bring her safely back to me. She holds the key to destroying the Light. We can use her hatred of the fugitive, and we can use the fugitive's love for her to destroy them all," the voice on the wind spoke again.

Zanah smiled with the knowledge of the plan that had eluded her until this moment, "Yes my Lord."

She spurred her horse forward, calling back to her warriors to prepare for battle. "Drive off the raiders, but only kill them if you have too. Save any nomads you can and assist them back to the other encampments," she ordered and descended the steep canyon slopes to the valley below.

CHAPTER FIVE

Lillian studied the area immediately around her. To one side flowed the half-frozen river that was the border of Halom itself, the other side the great Plains of Apistia where she had spent most of her young life. Across the meadowlands of Halom rose the Crystalline Mountains and Nomad Council stronghold where the clans now camped behind newly constructed walls. Fires burned nearer to where she stood, out in the cold darkness, marking the locations of her own clan's protective barriers. Walls that the Council had promised would keep the enemy away, walls that had proven useless against the Horde warriors and their war machines.

She needed a horse, she thought, and food for a journey. But she did not wish to go back to the fires where she knew both could be found. The Horde warriors were still everywhere, stealing and raping at will. But she had to secure a horse at least, so she tied the wet clothes around her and cautiously walked back toward the fires, keeping to the brush and out of the fire's glow.

She spotted the horses gathered within their corral across the fires. Closer to her lay several bodies of her clansmen, dead and stripped of their clothing. Lillian fought back tears of both sadness and rage and quickly looked away, focusing on the horses. She desperately wanted to see if her father was alive or dead, but at the same time did not want to look at the bodies for fear of seeing him lying there among the other members of her clan and family.

The Horde warriors piled the last of the clan's belongings on wagons as other warriors guarded the living clansmen who they had rounded up and surrounded. Soon they would round up the horses as well, so she knew that she did not have much time. There was a path through the trees that she knew well, that led around to the back of the corral, and she took it, walking as fast as she could without making any noise.

The path ended abruptly in a thicket of pine brush just outside of the railed fence. Lillian cautiously crawled under the brush through a wet blanket of snow and emerged just under the log rails. There were six horses standing in the corral, all of them known to her and would come to her by name if she called. But she dared not call, because one Horde warrior stood just across the corral from her, trying to bribe the horses with apples. She watched in frustration as one by one; the horses walked up to the man to take an apple from his outstretched hands.

And then suddenly one of the horses snorted and bolted across the corral toward Lillian. The others followed as something suddenly spooked them all. The sudden charge of the horses startled Lillian, and she scrambled backward to the fence, grabbing for the first horse that galloped by. She missed the halter and fell back against the railing, just as shadowed riders galloped by the fence. More warriors rode among the Horde, and a new battle was joined as the clansmen suddenly ran away as their guards turned to face a new threat.

Clashing swords echoed. Shadowed warriors fought from horseback, hacking downward into the Horde soldiers. Chaos of battle all around as warriors ran through the fire's orange glow, casting darkened shadows. Men ran all around Lillian as the horses panicked and broke through the gate. Lillian ran among the horses as well, seeing her chance to escape the chaos. Someone was attacking the Horde, but who? Maybe the Council had sent soldiers finally to save her people?

Lillian finally grasped a halter of one horse and quickly mounted as the mare galloped through the gate and out among the fighting soldiers. One grabbed for her, but she kicked him away and turned the horse toward the open prairie and drove the mare hard out into the darkness away from the burning encampment.

What was happening? She did not want to go back to see. Her fear of what the Horde would do to her if they caught her drove her forward even as she wondered if help had arrived to save them. Too little, too late, she thought. Her father had pleaded for the Council to send soldiers to help them, but they had been left to fend for themselves. Now her father was most likely dead, her home destroyed.

Lillian leaned forward against the horse, holding the mane tightly, allowing the horse to run on her instinct for escape. Lillian loved horses. She could handle them better than any of her family. She could ride better than even the clan's soldiers, and her ability gave her confidence that now that she was on horseback, no one could catch her.

Suddenly out in the darkness in front of her, she saw red beams of pale light and thought first of the dreaded Sahat that ruled the night. She pulled back on the horse's mane and finally slowed the mare's run down to a trot and then a full stop. Her breathing seemed to match the labored breathing of the mare. The fires were now over a mile off in the distance, the sound of battle only a very faint echo it seemed. The mare turned in a tight circle, and Lillian saw several more ghostly red lights behind her as well, the horses of the Sahat. But that could not be, she reasoned. The Sahat had suddenly disappeared from the land, and no one knew why. For several months since the Bene Elohim had first attacked the camp, scouts had reported that they had seen no roving bands of the Sahat, no fugitives wondering over the Plains of Apistia. The Bene Elohim had disappeared as well.

But horsemen were out in the night all around her. Lillian turned in the only direction where there were no lights, and just as she spurred her horse onward, the animal suddenly screamed in pain and turned hard to the right, knocking Lillian to the ground. Lillian fell, face forward, and quickly rolled out of the way of the falling horse. Warm fluid flowed over her face, running down her chest. She wiped the liquid from her and realized that it was blood from a wound in the horse's flank caused by a spear that protruded from the animal. The mare struggled in pain as Lillian crawled over to her old friend that lay her head down, still alive, but gasping for air, slowly losing consciousness as her life's blood flowed into the ground.

A flash of light momentarily blinded her, and a bronze warrior appeared out of the darkness or was it a Bene Elohim? Lillian could not tell at first and then she saw two Bene Elohim warriors running toward her. She scrambled away from the horse to run, when another rider suddenly appeared out of the darkness, the horse's eyes glowing red like the Sahat, but it was not a Sahat warrior riding the horse. The rider was a woman. She reached a gloved hand down to Lillian.

"Girl, grab hold!" the rider ordered.

But Lillian did not take the hand, too confused and afraid to do anything but run.

The rider cursed and turned the horse toward the oncoming warriors, and quickly parried the blow of the first one, knocking the man back.

She turned her horse back to Lillian, "Girl! If you want to live, grab hold. I will take you out of this place!" she ordered a second time.

Lillian grabbed the offered hand and was pulled behind the woman.

"Hold tight!" the woman ordered, and this time Lillian obeyed and the warrior sheathed her sword and turned the horse to face the oncoming warriors. But they were no longer anywhere to be seen. But out in the darkness, more horses galloped toward them.

CHAPTER SIX

The two women rode across the hills of Halom toward the Crystalline Mountains that glowed under the moon's light. For a while, their pursuers kept pace with them, but the Sahat horse was bred for battle and long-distance running, and after a while, there was no sign of any horsemen behind them. Lillian had to hold tightly to the woman who wore tightly fitted battle armor. Her long, thick hair blew outward and across Lillian's face for most of the ride and several times she had to pull the thick mane away from her so she could breathe. Finally, after miles of running across the prairie, the woman reined in her horse on a low rise overlooking a small lake with scattered trees, the water sparkling in the early morning light. She scanned the far hills, and they both listened carefully for any sound of horses running but heard nothing. The horse panted heavily, and even though it was freezing, sweat covered the animal.

Lillian was suddenly very cold and began to shake deep within her, not only from the cold but also because of the constant stress of the last night. Lillian studied the warrior who had saved her carefully, the long hair that smelled of lavender, small face, gold earrings, long, slender neck. She looked vaguely familiar, but Lillian was unsure.

"I think they have given up," the warrior spoke, breaking the spell her presence had cast over the younger girl.

"Let's rest a bit and build a small fire. I'm famished. Are you hungry?" the woman asked.

"Yea," Lillian answered, "and cold."

The warrior helped her down and then dismounted as well. She pulled her unruly hair away from her face and tied it back, revealing for the first time her face. She had bright green eyes. Lillian recognized her then. She had seen the woman once before at a clan gathering. She had been setting beside Archon Planos and the council leaders. With the recognition, Lillian suddenly realized she was in the presence of royalty and out of habit, bowed in both respect and fear.

"My Lady Zanah, I had no idea it was you. I am sorry."

Zanah dismissed her bow with a wave and smiled. "Child, you have nothing to be sorry for. It's okay, Lillian."

"You know my name, My Lady."

"Yes of course. I came to save you, child. I'm sorry we were not in time to save your family, but I'm glad that I caught up with you when I did. Lord Planos knows of your distress. He wishes to help you. But we will talk about this later. Now let's rest a bit and eat. Gather some wood for a fire, will you."

Zanah unsaddled the horse and brushed him down with dry grass, hobbled him and then let him loose to graze nearby. She then opened one of the saddlebags and pulled out some meat and herbs and placed them on a rock next to where Lillian had placed the sticks. Lillian saw that she had no flint or steel and wondered how she could start a fire. Zanah put the sticks around the food and with a wave of her hand, the fire suddenly flared up. She then added the rest of the sticks to the fire and with a gloved hand, withdrew the food from the fire that cooked miraculously and placed it on two plates that she had also pulled from the bag.

Lillian could not believe what she had seen. What type of magic was this, she asked herself?

"Here girl. Eat and get warm by the fire." Zanah ordered with a smile.

Lillian sat by the fire and accepted the food. Zanah also gave her a crystal cup full of water that she had pulled from the bag as well, which appeared too small to hold everything that she had seen the woman retrieve from it.

Lillian was hungrier than she ever remembered, but the terror of this past night weighed heavy in her thoughts. Her mind raced with everything that had transpired over the past few months. First, the camp had been attacked the first night they had crossed the river. Many had been killed. Jonathan had disappeared during the battle along with the fugitive girl Heather and the captive Bene Elohim. Where had they gone?

Her father had led the survivors to an encampment where they had to build walls to protect themselves. But that too had proven useless. Now her father was dead as well and most likely her entire family. Maybe even the whole clan. Suddenly the memories were too strong, the terrors too great, and Lillian began to cry, a deep, heartbroken cry of remorse, exhaustion, and hopelessness.

Zanah studied the girl carefully while Lillian cried. She felt no compassion for the girl. In fact, Zanah felt nothing either way for any of them. They were only pawns to her; beings created far beneath her status. They gave her pleasure just in the fact that she knew she could manipulate them at will, could control them, and ultimately could destroy them. That gave her the greatest pleasure of all.

In this case, however, it was imperative that the girl believed that Zanah truly cared for her, that she understood how she felt. Zanah would manipulate the girl's emotions until she totally controlled her with her magic of deception.

Zanah stepped across the fire and sat down beside Lillian. She took the plate of food from the girl and placed it on the ground and then pulled the girl close to her, holding her close and allowing her to cry. Lillian's chains covered her chest, intertwined with her clothing, seen only by Zanah because the deception of Halom hid them from sight. Unlike the fugitives of the Plains of Apistia who knew they were chained by the chains of death, the nomads believed that they had been set free from the ancient curse's bondage. They only came to a full realization of the trap they lived in when it was too late to do anything about it.

Zanah sighed as if it was a great struggle, in this case, to console the girl and spoke softly in Lillian's ear. "There, there child. Let it all out. It will be okay. I promise you that. I will protect you."

Lillian shook her head in acknowledgment.

"I am so very sorry that we came too late to save your family, but I promise that I will take you back with me so you can share your story. Lord Planos is a caring leader. He will fight to protect the clans. He will do all that he can to ensure that the Bene Elohim are destroyed."

Lillian nodded her head again, her crying now only a low moan, her hair covering her face, and she hugged Zanah deeply. Zanah smiled, not for the fact that she had offered comfort, but for the fact that she knew that she could control this girl to achieve Lord Planos' wishes.

"Thank you, My Lady. I have no place to go," Lillian looked up and smiled.

Zanah had bright green eyes that pulled her deep into some unfamiliar world with unfamiliar thoughts, unknown feelings. She knew the love of her father and her aunt Ruth and family. She had experienced a new, thrilling love of romance for a brief period with Jonathan. Now she felt a love that seemed to be a combination of both.

Her first impulse was to kiss the woman, the way she had once kissed Jonathan. She blushed at that and dismissed such a strange thought. Instead she wiped her eyes and pulled away, smiling, feeling comfort from Zanah's presence that she had never felt from anyone before, not even her father. But something about her stare had unnerved her. Something was not what it appeared to be. She was reminded of the first time she had kissed Jonathan quickly in the river when they had first reached the Hills of Halom, of how he had pulled her tightly to him later that night by the wagons and kissed her long and passionately. And then her world had been shattered by the attack of the Bene Elohim. Jonathan had betrayed them all by bringing the Light among them. But then again, she remembered how beautiful the Light had been as she gazed into its life.

Zanah knew that her magic over humans was tough if not impossible to overcome, especially when she could look deep into their soul through the gateway of her eyes. She had deceived many young men and women with her sexuality, but for some reason, just when she thought she had control, the girl had somehow rejected her advance. There was only one magic in the land that she knew of that could do that, but Lillian did not, could not have possessed that magic.

This one would take more manipulation to control, but no matter. Zanah took up the plate of food and placed it in Lillian's hands, "Here child. You need to eat."

Lillian took the food and began to eat. She was famished.

"We'll rest a bit and then be on our way. My home is only a half day's journey." Zanah commented as she walked back to her side of the small fire and sat to eat from her plate of food, watching the girl as she ate. The girl must have been exposed to the Light's magic while the fugitive had been with her. Its power over their mind could be substantial.

"So much has happened. I don't understand," Lillian suddenly broke the silence, "Jonathan said the Light had freed him of his chains, that it could free me as well. But I have already been freed of them."

Lillian felt down across her body, unknowingly rubbing her hands over the chains that wrapped around her. Zanah watched as she did this, delighted by the fact that the deception was so strong over her.

"He showed it to me once. It was so beautiful, but as the Light grew stronger, it hurt my eyes. For a moment I saw things that I had never seen before," she continued her story.

"I truly felt that I was falling in love with him. Father had said that his chains would be removed through the ceremony at the gathering and he could live with us. I was so happy. And then suddenly his chains were gone. How could that be? And the Bene Elohim were all around us, killing us. He tried to take me away, saying that it was all a lie and that the warriors were not Bene Elohim. I slapped him, screamed at him that he had betrayed us all, that he had brought the Bene Elohim to us."

Lillian began to cry again, "I thought he loved us. How could he do that? But just before I was pulled away from him by the mob, I saw something I had never seen before. For just a moment, I saw a shining form of a man standing behind him, or within him, or around him. I'm not sure. Who could that have been?"

Suddenly Zanah was alarmed by the girl's story. Somehow the Light had revealed itself to her. That was how she could have rejected her advances earlier.

"Lillian, I know that it has been hard for you. And what I am about to tell you will make it even harder, but you have to know the truth," Zanah began her lie, "Lord Planos knew about Jonathan. Remember the night of the attack. A group of nomadic warriors rode into your camp. They were sent to tell your father that Jonathan was a spy sent by the Bene Elohim to do exactly what you know to be true. He was sent to your camp to gain your trust and to be allowed to participate in the ceremony of the chains that have the true power to free your kind from the chains of death."

Lillian looked up into Zanah's eyes in surprise, pain and then anger. Good, Zanah thought. I can use that to manipulate her.

Zanah continued, "They were to arrest him and bring him back to the Council for trial before he could do great harm to all of us. The Bene Elohim must have been hiding nearby and attacked to save him from capture. They have taken him back to their land. They have gained control over the Plains of Apistia and send raiding parties over the hills from time to time, but not for long. We will avenge the death of your family and destroy the Light once and for all."

Lillian sat silently for a moment in total shock. What she had feared was true. Jonathan had betrayed them all.

"But the Light seemed so real. The vision of the man was not evil. He was the truth."

"I'm sorry child, but what you saw was not truth. It was very evil magic from ancient times. A magic that can deceive all of us if we are not careful. But you are a powerful one. You have a great destiny in you. You have the power to help us destroy the Light once and for all."

"How can I do anything?" Lillian asked.

"Jonathan targeted you, but you resisted. You overcame the magic. You can now destroy it. But don't worry about that now. Let's get some sleep. We are safe here. This afternoon I will take you to meet Lord Planos himself. He will be delighted to see the only nomad who has ever resisted the Light and won."

Lillian was suddenly very sleepy and soon was lost to the magic that had taken over her. She slept well, even though a part of her lay wide awake, knowing the truth, but bound by the lies, the chains drawing her strength away.

CHAPTER SEVEN

The nearby sounds of grazing horses and men talking woke Lillian up from her sleep. At first, she was alarmed, but then remembered where she was. Zanah stood by her horse talking with several warriors who were mounted. Nearby stood another horse, saddled and ready for their journey.

"Ah, you are awake," Zanah smiled down at her as Lillian stood up and dusted herself off.

"The soldiers will escort us to Archon Planos, and there is hope yet that some of your family may still be alive."

Lillian quickly reached for the horse's reins, "What do you mean? My family, alive!"

"Maybe child. They have told me that they were able to chase off the attackers last night and many of your clan are even now traveling to the Council headquarters where they will be safe."

Lillian could not believe this. Her family could be alive!

Lillian pulled the horse closer to her. He was a spotted black and white with shaggy hair and a long, black mane that had a wild way about him, but Lillian was used to horses, loved them, and had never met one that she could not ultimately tame. This one pranced a bit around her as she held the reins tightly. She pulled his head down to her, rubbing his neck with the other hand and talked to him softly. She looked directly into his eyes, and soon he nudged her gently and turned submissively to one side.

"Good boy," Lillian praised the horse, patting him gently as Zanah and the escorts looked on.

"I'm impressed young lady," Zanah commented, genuinely approving of the girl's ability.

Lillian mounted the horse and turned him to face the others, "Thank you, My Lady. I grew up with horses. My father always said that I held a special power over them, even the worst ones."

At the sudden memory of her father, Lillian looked away.

"Think positive, child. There is still hope that your father is alive," Zanah commented and then spurred her horse onward.

With a jump, Lillian's horse quickly followed as the escort fanned out both to the front and back of them. Zanah had said that they would reach her home in just a few hours and that her clan was on their way as well. There was still hope.

The group rode for an hour across grassland spotted with occasional trees and crossed by several small streams that flowed merrily through rocky channels. Lillian had never traveled through the land before and was totally unfamiliar with her surroundings. Zanah had said that they were going toward the Crystalline Mountains, but there was no sign of the majestic, rocky mountain, only endless meadows of thick, winter grass and shaded glens covered in snow.

And then, as if by magic, the towering cliffs revealed themselves on the horizon as the horses trotted up to a small rise that, for miles, had hidden what lay behind. A thin, dark green band of spruce covered the lower slopes of the mountain range before giving way to ledges of gray rock and bright red sandstone that glowed in the afternoon sun. A massive cathedral of cliffs and broken crags reached upward into a thick layer of fog that forever covered the upper slopes that blew across the southern hills like smoke from a wildfire, snow, and ice glistening in the massive cracks and crevices.

The group stopped along the vantage point to look in wonder at the mystery that lay before them. For her entire life, Lillian had always marveled at the site of the mountain range that formed the western boundary of the Hills of Halom, but she had never seen the mountains from this side. For a moment the fog separated, and she thought she could see an even further range of blue mountains between the gap. For her entire life, she had been told that the mountain range was the end of the world with only blackness behind the barrier. But from this vantage point, she could, for just a moment, see a whole new land of forested mountain slopes that lay in a gray-blue haze.

Zanah pulled a telescope from the saddlebag and inspected the slopes and hills below them. She lowered the lens and handed it to Lillian, "Look there Lillian. I can see the nomad camps. We should be there in a short time."

With her naked eye, Lillian only saw the grasslands, but when she gazed through the lens, the multicolored nomad tents shone vividly against the horizon. Tiny people were building a wooden palisade around the encampment with watchtowers. A group of horsemen and wagons were approaching the tent city, cattle, and horses following behind. That would be another nomad band approaching. Maybe her own family was there among them, she thought.

She swept her gaze across the encampment to the forested slopes and towering cliffs, where for the first time she noticed battlements, towers, and walls built directly into cliff walls rising just above the forest. But what astonished her more than anything was the blue mountain range that lay beyond the cliffs.

Zanah was talking to the escort and did not notice that Lillian had edged herself forward in the saddle as she zoomed the lens in on the distant mountain range. Now through the foggy mist, she saw dark, forested slopes, open mountain meadows, a glistening waterfall and then small individual columns of white smoke floating lazily upward. At the base of the smoke, appeared a small village of wooden structures covering a meadow. What a beautiful, peaceful place, she thought.

"My Lady, what is that beyond the cliffs?" she asked.

At first, Zanah did not seem to notice what she said, "What do you mean Lillian? There is nothing beyond the Crystalline Mountains, only blackness. A great void where no man goes," Zanah lied.

She knew what lay behind the mountains, as all the Archons knew.

"But I see forested mountains and a waterfall. There is a village there."

Zanah took the lens to look for herself and saw precisely what the girl was describing. How could that be? There was a great gash in the fog that always hid the country beyond from anyone's sight. But now Zanah could see the kingdom beyond the mountain range, a domain that her kind had closed off to the Shadow Realm long ago.

Zanah knew she had to do something quickly to close the gap, but even her magic was not strong enough to do that. She had to alert Archon Planos that something wrong had occurred, that the portals they had shut seemed to have opened, but how? She continued to gaze through the lens and chanted silently, waving her hand by her side and as she did so, the fog thickened as if painted on the sky and the mountain range disappeared. She then moved her hand again, and the village appeared again, but at this time it lay on this side of the cliffs below the forest.

"I don't see what you're talking about," Zanah commented, "Wait, there it is. I see the village now, but it lies at the base of the mountain in the gap."

She handed the lens back to Lillian, "See, there, just to the right of the fortress in the rock. Lord Planos told me he was expanding the village because of the increased number of clans coming back."

Lillian looked through the lens again. Now she could only see the thick fog covering the highest mountain peaks and the village below the gap as Zanah had described. There was nothing else, nothing she had thought she had seen before. But she was sure of what she had seen.

"You see what I'm talking about?" Zanah asked.

Lillian was not sure, but she could not refute what she was now looking at. There was the village that she had seen before at the base of the mountain, the majestic and foreboding mountain range behind it.

"Yea. I see it. The fog blew across the mountain and confused me." Lillian answered and handed the telescope back. But she knew exactly what she had first seen. Why it had changed, she could not understand, but something inside told her not to say any more about it.

Satisfied with the girl's answer, Zanah placed the lens back in her saddlebags and ordered the group to continue. But as they rode down the hill toward the distant camp, Zanah could still see through her magic spell to an open portal in the mountain gap to the hidden kingdom beyond the mountains. Something wrong had happened. She looked over at the girl riding beside her. Could she have something to do with what was going on? So many things had changed since the Archon Krino had disappeared. The girl had been exposed to the Light when the fugitive had escaped. Unknowingly she had been able to withstand her magic spell the night before. Maybe the Light had somehow given her some power to see past the magic.

"I have the girl," Zanah spoke in a tongue that only Archon Planos could hear.

Planos stood at the window overlooking Halom. He could see Zanah and the others riding toward him even though they were still several miles away.

"Good. Bring her to me. Her clan is either dead or taken away to a place where she will never see them again."

"I offered her hope that she may yet see them alive."

"Hatred is a stronger incentive, don't you think?'

"I presume so. Why don't I show her what her lover is capable of? Then we can turn her totally to us."

Planos could read Zanah's thoughts as she could his even from great distances. They were a pair, yet they were also the same.

"Yes, yes, you do that. Then bring her to me."

"One more thing, my love. Lillian saw through the portal to The Kingdom. How is that possible?"

Planos thought for a moment before answering. He had no answer. Nor did Zanah.

The group galloped past the first nomad tents scattered outside the palisade, the people staring as they rode by. The entire time, Lillian thought of what she had viewed through the telescope before it had suddenly changed. The thought of land beyond the Crystalline Mountains went against everything that she had ever been taught. There was only the Plains of Apistia and the Hills of Halom, the Forest of Basar and the Crystalline Cliffs. Three words jumped out from the darkest recesses of her mind, virtue, peace, joy. She could not understand why she equated the mountain range to those words, but the vision she saw cast a troubled cloud over her, like something was not what it appeared to be, that something was speaking to her from some far off place. Something lay just out of her grasp, of her comprehension, of her ability to see correctly.

But what she saw as the group stopped by a circle of wagons she did fully understand. Zanah dismounted and walked forward to the first wagon. Lillian knew the instant that she saw the cart that it belonged to her father. She quickly dismounted and ran past Zanah to look in the wagon itself. It was empty except for the body of her father, covered in blood from multiple stab wounds.

What she feared to be true had happened. She screamed and climbed into the wagon, reached and pulled the body over to look at the face of her father. He was dead, his body already stiff, the glazed eyes staring outward into nothingness.

Lillian slumped back against the seat, heaving, crying intensely before looking past the wagon to the next one. Bodies filled the next wagon as well. She climbed out and ran to the second wagon and then to a third and fourth wagon, all full of bodies of her clan, murdered by the Bene Elohim.

Zanah caught up to her then and placed a hand on her shoulder. Lillian spun violently to lash out but stopped when she saw who was standing there behind her.

"What happened? You said that they may yet be alive. They're dead, all dead!" Lillian began to cry again.

"I'm sorry child. They were attacked again on their way to safety. This time they were all killed." Zanah replied.

Lillian slumped forward and passed out.

CHAPTER EIGHT

Total blackness lay all around. Lillian stood in a void where nothing seemed to exist. She had a lingering feeling that there had been more of something before, but she could not fathom what that something was. It was as if a part of her existence had been torn away from her, that she once had been whole, but now she was not. She felt down her body and realized with sudden dread that she stood totally naked in the blackness. She heard no sound, felt nothing but herself. She realized that she was not standing on anything, her bare feet touching nothing beneath her. She stood suspended in total nothingness.

Panic welled up within her, and her breathing increased as her heart raced. She reached out around her, but there was nothing. She cried out to the darkness and realized that she could not even hear her own screams for help. She had to get control of herself. This had to be some terrible nightmare, but to her, it seemed to be real.

And something moved around her in the blackness. She heard whispers, voices that were far off, but coming closer. She smelled the familiar odor of horses, smoke, sweat, and blood. And then the whispers became shouts and screams. Metal clashed against metal, war cries rang out in the darkness and all around her men fought, but she still could not see anything.

What was happening? She thought. Fear replaced the panic, yet she could do nothing but exist in the blackness. Swords and battle axes passed over her head, and she jumped away each time she felt the cold steel move against her naked skin. Each time she fully expected to feel the pain of terrible wounds, but the blades only glanced against her, passed over her. She heard the sickening sounds of impact, the screams of pain, and the cries of death.

And then slowly the images gained substance around her as small amounts of light pushed back the darkness, and with horror, she realized that she was in the middle of the first attack of the Bene Elohim by the river Dolios when the clan had first entered the Hills of Halom. Lillian saw herself standing over the body of her cousin Cristina, holding a knife and screaming as horsemen rode past her. And then Jonathan suddenly pushed his way through the crowd and shouted at her, "Lillian, you must come with me quickly. We have to leave this place!"

Lillian watched as Jonathan grabbed at her, but she resisted.

"Jonathan! They killed Cristina. The horrid Bene Elohim killed her. They will kill us all!"

"No Lillian, you are wrong. This is an illusion. Nothing is as it appears!'

Lillian watched as Jonathan took her by the hand. He stood before her without the chains, and a beautiful translucent light glowed all over him and around him. Lillian slapped him hard across the face, "'Look what you have done!"

Jonathan ignored the slap but pulled her toward him, and for a moment, the Light enveloped them both, before the mob separated her and pulled her away. The Light pulled away from her as well, and Lillian stood amazed as she watched the scene before her. Standing behind Jonathan amid the Light was a man, holding his arms outward toward her.

All vanished before her, and she stood again in total blackness, but there was a presence standing somewhere with her, somewhere just out of reach. She did not fear the presence but knew that something was there somewhere in the darkness. And then she heard.

"THIS IS ALL AN ILLUSION. THIS DOMAIN WAS NEVER MEANT TO BE. THE TRUE KINGDOM IS OUT THERE."

Lillian awoke suddenly, visibly shaken be the dream. She lay on a bed in a room, warm covers over her. She looked around her, confused. She remembered seeing the bodies, the wagons and then the strange nightmare that caused her to shake inwardly.

Her family was dead, killed by the Bene Elohim. All that she had been was now destroyed. And Jonathan had been the cause. Her family had saved him from the desert, had mended him back to health. They had trusted him. She had loved him. And according to Zanah, he had brought the enemy to them. Jonathan had betrayed them all. Zanah had told her that she could help destroy the Light once and for all and that Archon Planos would help her avenge her family's death.

But the horrid dream confused her. Something deep lay just out of her reach. The voice had said the real kingdom is out there. Out where she thought? What is the illusion and what is the truth? She had seen a distant land where no land should be.

"VIRTUE, PEACE, JOY"

What voice rang out from some remote mountaintop, it seemed, but then again from within her own mind? Lillian shook her head and pulled her errant hair back from her face. The stress of the past few days was too much, she thought. She seemed to be going mad with voices and nightmares that she had never experienced before. And since the first attack, the constant thought that she was only half a person, that a part of her very being had somehow been pulled from her drove her toward insanity.

She set up on her bed, and the covers fell away from her, revealing the fact that she now wore a white cotton dress. Her tattered clothes lay on a couch by the bed. Her room appeared to be on an upper floor of some structure because she saw a balcony across the room from the bed with treetops level with the railing outside the door. Outside, the sun shone from a beautiful, bright blue sky. She stood up totally confused even more as she walked over to the glass door and opened it, revealing a warm day, full of sunshine. A soft, warm breeze blew across her face. The trees below her were alive and green with fresh summer leaves. Birds flew across the sky. Others sang merrily from the trees themselves.

It was late winter, she thought. How could the trees be covered in leaves, the day so warm and the place full of songbirds? Lillian leaned over the railing slightly and looked below her and to both sides. Her room appeared to be on the third floor of a large stone structure. There were many balconies on each side of her as well as others below her. Across the landscape below grew massive oak trees with gravel walking trails below that meandered through manicured gardens with colorful flowers, fountains, greenery and stone statues. The sight was breathtaking.

Lillian looked outward past the park and was rewarded by the view of a meadow of rolling hills that spread outward toward the distant mountain range of granite cliffs and towering spires that rose upward into the gray clouds. She recognized the familiar cliffs of the Crystalline Mountain range.

And then floating on the breeze, the faint sound of harp music played, and Lillian thought she heard laughter and whispered voices from the garden below, but she saw no one.

Lillian jumped at the sound of a soft knock on the door to her room. She turned as a young girl hesitantly stepped into the half-open door. The girl could not have been over 18 years old, short of stature with curly brown hair and a small elfish face with dark eyes.

She smiled and curtseyed slightly, "I am sorry to bother you mistress, but it is close to lunch time, and Lord Planos has asked me to see if you need anything. He wishes for you to meet him outside on the veranda where lunch will be served."

Lillian looked at herself in the mirror. Her long hair was a mess, but the dress looked fine on her, and she was barefooted.

The girl anticipated her question, "There is a wash basin there to freshen up and several pairs of shoes that you can use."

Lillian looked across the row of women's shoes on the floor next to her pair of leather riding boots that she usually wore. She overlooked the slippers and picked a soft pair of moccasins. The girl waited patiently as Lillian tried on the shoes which fit and were very comfortable. She then combed out her long hair and tamed it somewhat by pulling it back from her face in one long ponytail. Satisfied by her appearance, she walked to the door.

"This way mistress," the girl motioned with her hand and Lillian followed her from the room.

They walked down a long, darkened hallway; the walls built of granite rock. The hall was lit by small torches stationed in small gaps in the wall until the hall turned to the right and suddenly was illuminated by the sunlight shining through large glassed windows that overlooked the park below. After climbing down a curved stairway, they exited the building, and Lillian found herself on a large porch built of cedar and rock. The whole place was magical with beautifully constructed archways, banisters, and balconies.

Across the yard from the porch, a large veranda built of cedar stood among a grove of large oak trees. A large table sat under the shelter. There were also several couches and chairs situated around and within the structure itself. The table appeared to be set for a large party with crystal plates and drinking glasses. And to one side of the table, a bar was covered with all types of food, more food than Lillian had ever seen. The soft breeze carried the wondrous aroma of meats, and freshly baked bread and Lillian suddenly realized just how hungry she was.

Lillian stopped at the sight before her, and the young girl did as well. Lillian glanced at the girl who stood a few steps to her side.

"Welcome my dear," a voice spoke, and Lillian looked back to the veranda.

She was surprised at the sight of a large, robed man sitting at the head of the table and Zanah, dressed in a beautiful green gown sitting next to him. Several uniformed servants were busily preparing the lunch to be served. How could that be? Lillian thought. No one had been there just a moment before. She turned to the girl again, and she was gone. Lillian looked around her, but there was no sight of the young girl, where only seconds before she had been standing immediately beside her.

"Come dear," Zanah spoke, "you must be famished."

Lillian was hungry, and the food smelled and looked delicious. Lillian stepped up into the veranda and took a seat held open for her by one of the servants. Without saying a word, the servant placed the food on her plate and poured her a cup of dark, red wine. Lillian sat there, not knowing what to do or say, the situation awkward to her.

"Lillian, this is Lord Planos, our protector, and Archon of this land," Zanah announced.

Lillian looked up at the man who smiled widely at her, "It's okay child. I am truly blessed to meet your acquaintance. Zanah has spoken very highly of you. You are welcome in my home. I am truly sorry for all that has happened to you and your family. But we will not be disturbed by such tragedies at this time. My home is a welcome place, a soothing place where you can lose yourself and find peace and joy, even when all around there is pain and sadness."

"Thank you, my Lord. I have already felt the peace you speak of," Lillian responded.

"Good, good. Now let's eat, and after lunch, we will talk more about how we can avenge the wrongs done against you."

Lillian observed Lord Planos as she ate. He appeared to be a young man. However, something about him seemed ancient as well. His blue eyes sparkled in the sun's light, and he had a full head of hair and thick black beard speckled with gray. Lillian could not believe that she sat at his table, eating lunch with him. For her entire life, she had been taught that Archon Planos was the clan's protector, that he gave the clan freedom from the chains of death through the initiation of the chains ceremony done in a secret place each year. She had been a child when her chains had been removed and only remembered fire and smoke in a dark place and a bearded man standing over her in the shadows. Suddenly she knew that the man had been Lord Planos himself, the only other time in her life that she had ever seen him close.

Zanah, on the other hand, usually appeared at clan meetings and ceremonies, always accompanied by a giant warrior who followed her everywhere she went. No one understood the relationship between Lord Planos and Lady Zanah, she thought. Were they husband and wife, or brother or sister, or just close friends? They jointly ruled over their kingdom, Archon Planos from his headquarters, and Lady Zanah with the people. They ruled the clans through the council elders who lived all year in Halom.

But that had all changed since the Bene Elohim had invaded the land, she thought. Now the Council had no power at all. The Archons ruled the clan directly and had them stay in Halom behind fortified encampments. They were free of their chains, she thought, but they were no longer free.

And why do you think that is, she asked herself? Jonathan has betrayed your family. He is the reason your family is dead. The Light he brought into your camp opened a way for the Bene Elohim to attack. Jonathan has betrayed us all. Lillian thought to herself.

Lillian did not notice that Zanah had not eaten anything, but the entire time had been staring directly at her. She whispered lies into the girl's thoughts and could feel Lillian's mind bending to her control. She continued to lead her into a deeper world of deception and then suddenly something barred her further entrance. Some unknown force kept her from fully controlling the young girl's thoughts. Just like the time by the fire on the first night.

"THE TRUE KINGDOM IS OUT THERE."

A voice spoke to Lillian, and startled, she dropped her fork and looked to both Zanah and Planos, but they appeared not to have heard the voice.

Zanah could not understand what had suddenly broken the spell. It would take more time, she thought.

"You can't control this one, my dear," Archon Planos spoke directly to her mind from his as he continued to eat. He had noticed as well and had heard the voice as a whisper far off but could not tell what had been said.

Zanah did not answer the challenge. She would work her magic at another time.

Archon Planos motioned for the servants, and immediately they began to clear away the dishes. Other servants appeared from behind the wall and helped. In just a few minutes they had removed all evidence that lunch had ever been eaten in the veranda and disappeared behind the wall as Planos waited patiently.

"So, my dear, you are Captain Connelly's daughter?" he asked.

"Yes, My Lord," Lillian responded, the very mention of her father's name bringing back the incredible anguish of his loss, the haunting memories of seeing his vacant eyes staring up at her from the wagon.

"I cannot imagine the pain you must be going through, but you have to find a way to push past it, to channel the pain, to turn it into a resolve to do whatever you can to destroy the evil that killed your family," Planos stated.

Lillian looked up at the man, then over to Zanah, "But what can I do, my Lord?"

Zanah answered her question, "Lillian, Jonathan was sent by the Bene Elohim as a spy to gain access to the council through your clan, and He targeted you. He tried to deceive you. The magic of the Light is powerful, but you were able to withstand its power. You told me yourself that you saw the Light. He showed it to you and yet you were able to overcome its' draw. "

"I don't understand what I saw. I believed in him. I thought that I could love him. He was to be free of his chains and then father said he could become one of us. It was as if we had always been together, that he was a part of me and I him. How can that be?"

Zanah smiled, "That is the part of the deception of the Light. But look at yourself. You're free of the chains of sin. Your clan has always been free of the chains, through the ceremony of the chains. The lie of the Light is that it has the power to remove the fugitive's chains, but you know in your heart that this is not true. You saw the Bene Elohim attack your family on the night that you saw the Light, did you not?'

Lillian remembered seeing the Bene Elohim warriors killing her family.

"Yes."

"Then you know the truth child," Archon Planos stated, "And you must use that truth to help us rid the realm of this evil once and for all. Jonathan must be destroyed. He used you to gain access to the clan, but you now know the truth. You have the power to overcome the Light's magic, and you can now deceive him."

Zanah suddenly smiled as she stared into the eyes of Planos. What an excellent plan you have conceived, she thought.

"Thank you, my love" Planos answered her silently.

Lillian thought for a moment. So much had happened. She had witnessed so many things the past few days. The dreams, the vision of a land beyond the cliffs, the voice that cried from beyond the fog. But all of that was a mystery, a shadow of truth. She did not understand any of those things, but she did understand that her family was dead, that the Light was responsible and that somehow, even though it still panged her to think so, Jonathan had betrayed her love.

"What can I do, my Lord?' she asked

"Get him to give you the Light," Planos answered.

CHAPTER NINE

The morning sun shined brightly even though partially hidden behind the ever-present fog that covered the highest rocky spires of the canyon walls that surrounded the valley that Archon Planos and Zanah called their home. Lillian had been awakened earlier by the young servant girl by her customary knock on the door and request for her to come to the veranda for breakfast as she had done for the past two days since arriving at the home. Lillian tried to talk with the girl, but she would only smile and say that breakfast was waiting. And then she would quietly disappear back into the house, not to be seen again until she would find Lillian and summon her to supper. Two servants would set her table and patiently wait until she finished eating before cleaning the table without a word. And they too would disappear until supper was served at night.

What a strange place this was, Lillian thought, but beautiful as well. Zanah had eaten with her each evening, but Archon Planos had not been seen since the first time. Zanah had spent some time going over the plan to get the Light from Jonathan, and the more Lillian talked with the woman, the more she realized that Jonathan truly was the reason why her family was dead. A resentment bordering on pure hatred swelled within her, not so much against Jonathan, but entirely against the Bene Elohim. And if capturing Jonathan was the way to destroy the Bene Elohim as Zanah had said, then that was what she would do. But deep within, she still did not want to hurt Jonathan, hoping perhaps that he was not a willing participant, but trapped by the Bene Elohim into doing their bidding.

Zanah and Planos had not been to breakfast this morning. When asked, one of the servants said they were with the nomads, and she could go anywhere in the valley she wished as long as she did not leave, and that they would return in a few days time. Lillian knew of only one way out of the valley, a tunnel through the rock wall that was guarded by two warriors. She was a prisoner in the valley.

Zanah had said that her part in the plan was to wait in the valley until Jonathan came to free her. The story would be let out to him, wherever he was, that she was a prisoner and wished to be free. He was sure to come, Zanah had said, and when he did, she was to get the Light from him. Once free from the Light, Jonathan could, in turn, be saved from the Light's evil influence. Zanah had told her that once free of the Light, she would help Jonathan as well. The Bene Elohim only had power in the realm if someone had possession of the Light. Once the Light was destroyed, the Bene Elohim would vanish from the kingdoms and the clans would be free from their constant attacks. Life could go on as before.

But not really, Lillian thought as she walked among the garden paths. Her family was dead. Something deep within her had been torn from her, but she could not understand what it was. Something was missing, something indistinguishable and just out of reach of her intellectual ability to reach it. So many things had happened to her these past few weeks, things she did not understand. She trusted both Planos and Zanah, as her upbringing had taught her to do. They had saved her, brought her to this beautiful oasis, and believed in her as no one had done before.

Birds flew among the trees above her, darting in and out of the foliage, their multicolored feathers reflecting the sun's light. Deer fed on the lush grass by the stream that meandered merrily through the valley toward the far distant rocky cliffs. Such a peaceful place this was, she thought. It was so different from the Plains of Apistia where the nomads traveled each year. It was even more beautiful than the Hills of Halom where the nomads now encamped. She knew that out there, winter still held a grip on the land, but here in this place, spring in all its glory shined forth with every wildflower, every bird, every blade of grass and fluttering leaf.

As she walked, Lillian breathed in the intoxicating aroma of wildflowers and spruce trees. She lost herself entirely in the grandeur of the valley and soon forgot all about her past life outside the walls. She danced among the flowers. She climbed the trees like she had done years ago as a child. She watched in awe as the deer walked up to her with no fear and allowed her to pet them. All around her was beauty and peace.

But she had no idea that the entire time, someone watched from the mountain cliffs.

"You had little faith in my ability my love. The girl thinks she has been here only a few days, but it has been months," Zanah stated, glancing over to her counterpart that stood to one side of her.

Archon Planos smiled, "We shall see. But your enchantment seems to have worked so far. She totally believes she is playing among The Garden."

"They always do, my love," Zanah answered, "Do you wish to send the messenger now?"

"I think so. Send one of your warriors as a fugitive to the river with the news that the girl is our captive and that there is a way to the valley. When he gives her the Light to convert her, we will be ready," Planos ordered.

Zanah turned and kissed Planos lightly on the cheek, and both were suddenly lost among the mist that was the fog but not before looking once more on the handiwork that Zanah's magic had worked on the young girl.

MACKENZIE'S JOURNAL
DAY ONE

Father, what would you have me do? What should I pray for? Father, I need a fresh ENCOUNTER with you. I starve for more of your presence in all my life. Open doors of opportunity, open doors of ministry, open doors of relationships. I seek your wisdom, your heart, your righteousness, your peace, your joy. The Kingdom of God within me.

The rain falls, each drop separate, but all together as one. The weight would be too much to bear if it all came down in one massive sheet of water. But the same amount can fall in small, unique droplets and the world is not crushed by the weight but awakens to new life. That is the same with your presence at times, I think.

I seek justice, but for who. It is not mine to seek. Justice belongs only to you, my God. Give me your life, God. Your strength, your will, your kingdom. Arise in me in glory. Live in me in grace. Flow through me in power. Reside in the recesses of my soul.

What is the key to your kingdom? What is the source of your power? Your love? Your strength? Your compassion? Your ability? You are the source of all that is life.

Then live fresh in me. Burn through me with holy fire. Quench the longing of my soul. Birth the life in me that I was meant to live.

The sun casts shadows across the land, revealing the hidden things, and then they disappear as if they had never been. The same as with your spirit across my soul, I think.

God hold me, strengthen me, give me wisdom. I seek your wisdom. A new revelation of who I am in you. Who you are in me. Breathe new life, a new man, a new temple, a new throne. Make me a habitation of your spirit where there are no longer shadows, but only the truth of what is there to see.

Cleanse my mind of past things. Reveal yourself through me.

The keys of the kingdom abide in you. Therefore, the keys to the kingdom are you and only you. My life is yours to live. My soul is your garden to till, to nourish, to plant and to harvest.

The rain falls in small droplets upon my soul. The sun drives away shadows and reveals the truth. Your seed grows; your presence invades my soul, pushing all away until only your glory remains.

CHAPTER TEN

    The great river roared with power and fury, the water frothy and white-capped, swirling, ghostly specters at times reaching outward. Just as the first time he had saw the river, Peter thought to himself as he stood on a rocky outcrop overlooking the river crossing. Once only marked by a single white rock, the passage was now well marked and guarded by two connecting stone round towers, one on each side of the river with a connecting walkway reaching between the towers over the water itself. Archers stood to watch in each tower as well as along the walkway, always vigilant of roving bands of desert marauders that at times would attack the crossing to destroy it.

    The afternoon was beautiful, the sky a bright blue with smoky, white clouds drifting slowing past, the setting sun painting the clouds with lavender and red hues. Eagles flew high above, floating on wind currents, circling ever higher toward the clouds.

    Across the river, the growing village of Soteria lay situated within the meadow beyond the vast forest that grew along the river's bank. Since the Apostolos Or had defeated Archon Krino, all the fugitives of the Plains of Apistia suddenly found their chains removed. They now flocked to the crossing to be united with the Soterians. A strong army was forming that would one day be able to destroy all the Archons of the Shadow Realm, but only when the Apostolos Or gave the command.

    Peter liked to set on the precipice each afternoon to watch the crossing below, the beautiful valley across the river, the peaceful village, and the glorious sunset. He thought about all that had happened over the past few months. The first he had seen the crossing, Jonathan had led them, there had been a great battle, Krino had been destroyed and his friend and captain, Patrick had given his life so that Jonathan, Heather and himself could live and cross to the other side.

    "What you thinking?" a female voice called from behind the cluster of rocks.

Peter turned in the direction of the voice and was rewarded by the sight of his soul mate, her long, blond hair entirely covering her young face as she leaned over to pull herself up the last rock and jumped over the ledge to land next to Peter as he watched. Heather leaned over and kissed Peter and then sat next to him, handing him a canteen full of water from the springs of Soteria.

"I figured you would be here, love," the girl remarked, "You worried about him?"

Peter shook his head.

"Yea, me too, but we must trust the Light that he will know what to do," Heather responded as she pulled back Peter's thick hair from his face, revealing a short beard over a weather-beaten, tanned face, scarred in one place from a battle wound years before. The disfigurement did not bother her at all. To Heather, Peter was the most beautiful man in the realm.

Peter reached around Heather's slight form and pulled her next to him, and they sat together, enjoying the ever-changing view below them as they did almost every day.

"With everything that has happened, he seems to lose himself more every day in deep thought. He walks the ridgeline for hours, at times staring toward the distant horizon across the plains," Peter commented.

"He misses her more and more each day," Heather responded and placed her head against Peter's chest.

"Jonathan still blames himself for not taking Lillian when he escaped, but there was nothing he could do. Malak said it was not time," Peter said and then kissed Heather lightly on the head, breathing in the aroma of her hair and thinking of how Jonathan had saved Heather from certain death on that same night.

"He saved us all, Peter. He shared the Light with each of us, and we are free because of him. Why he could not save Lillian as well, I still do not understand. But I know that if he had disobeyed Malak's orders and tried to rescue Lillian, I would have been killed by the Sahat. He found me hiding under the wagon during the attack and helped me to escape. In fact, I think if he had been disobedient, all of us would have been killed." Heather sighed heavily thinking about what she had just said. "But still, it is so sad that Jonathan is so lost when his sacrifice so blesses you and me," she continued.

"He told me the other day that he felt as if something had been torn from him, that he was only a half person," Peter remarked, "And now we know that she has been captured and held prisoner and he will go to her. He must save her, or he will never be whole."

"That's true love, Peter. Just think of us. I could not imagine not being with you."

"I know, love. I feel the same way about you, but Malak says that what Jonathan is going through is not love, although love is a part of it. He says that Jonathan must be reconciled with himself and her for us all to be whole. We, after all, are all just a part of his story. The entire Shadow Realm hangs in the balance by what must be done."

Heather laughed, "Malak always talks in riddles. What does he mean by that?"

"I really don't know, and I'm glad that we are not required to understand. Only Jonathan needs to. Our job is to ready the forces, and when the time comes, we will destroy the Shadow Realm once and for all."

The two fell silent and reflected on the past few day's events. A fugitive had arrived by the tower and told a story of how he had witnessed a girl taken prisoner by the Council of the Nomads. They had accused her of befriending a fugitive who had brought the Bene Elohim into the realm. They blamed her for what had taken place across the Shadow Realm and had taken her to the Crystalline Mountains where she was jailed. She was to be executed at the next ceremony of chains by Archon Planos himself. When asked by Jonathan who the girl was, he had told him that she was the only daughter of Captain Connelly.

"Peter, do you know this Archon Planos?" Heather asked.

"I only saw him a few times. He travels with a witch called Zanah everywhere he goes. He is the protector of the Nomads and rules over the Hills of Halom. Patrick knew him better. He was said to be a shape shifter, a shaman, a deceiver. Patrick never trusted him. In fact, that was why we were searching for the Light on the night you were rescued. We were trying to capture Malak and use him to discredit Planos."

"Can Jonathan defeat him?"

"I don't know Heather, but he has to. Or else all we have achieved will be for nothing," Peter answered.

"But why doesn't Malak go with him. The Bene Elohim were always there with us before. Why can't they go now?" Heather asked, worried.

"Heather, I don't fully understand, but Jonathan is the Apostolos Or over the Shadow Realm. The Bene Elohim were sent to the realm to make sure the Apostolos Or was found, and the Light was activated. I think now they wait to see if Jonathan can fully command the Light's power."

They fell silent as they watched the sudden commotion below them by the river. A rider crossed the river and at the tower, he turned to wave to those that stood on the other side. He then turned the horse and looked up to the cliffs where he knew Peter and Heather sat together each evening. He saluted them in farewell and then rode off down the trail by the river, toward the Plains of Apistia.

The two Bene Elohim, Malak and Nasar, stood by the river, watching as Jonathan rode away toward the Plains of Apistia. They would have both gladly traveled with him, but they knew that at present, it was no longer their responsibility. Jonathan must fight his own battles for him to be made entirely whole. Behind the veil that was the Shadow Realm, the Kingdom waited, and their job in this realm was over.

MACKENZIE'S JOURNAL
DAY TWO

I live in this world, in this day, in time…..
Your glory God. Take the doubt away. You are truly in my tomorrow. I live in this day and this day is eternity if you are within it, which you are. Therefore, my soul is an eternal one because you are eternal.

There is a challenge to all things under the sun. Challenge comes on the wind, blows on the sea, flows in the air, drives men away, pushes past our humanity and splits the rule of God. Or so it seems.

But light only moves forward and breaks through the darkness. Light attacks the challenge of mankind and sears away the doubts of man. And only the Kingdom remains in the garden of the soul that is safe and secure in the eternity that is the day in which we live.

I cry to a God that knows no boundaries. I pray to a Father, a Father of love. The Eternal One. My needs are great it seems, but what are they to an Eternal One who is beyond all that we know, all that we are, and all that we are to be.

Today I hunger. The fear is just beyond my grasp, floating on the horizon of my soul, flirting with time and space. It dances a seductive dance, which if I yield will pull me back into time itself. But today is eternal in my Father. The fear and doubt are only shadows cast by time. The light shines, but in the mist of rain, no shadows appear.

God is eternal and His will is truth. The Kingdom is in the present, and the present in the Kingdom is eternity.

CHAPTER ELEVEN

Jonathan traveled along the forested trail for several hours into increased darkness as the sun melted behind the canyon walls behind him. The forest darkened very quickly with the disappearance of the sun, but the Light around his neck illuminated the trail. His horse trotted along the trail quickly, and Jonathan quickly became lost in his thoughts, fully trusting the horse to follow the path that the Light exposed.

He no longer feared the darkness as he had always done so before the chains had disappeared from around him. The dreaded Sahat had once ruled the night, destroying fugitives whose time had come, but since his victory over Krino, the Sahat had disappeared from the realm. Although no longer fearing death from the Sahat, the Shadow Realm itself still held power over Jonathan in a way that he could not fully understand. He knew that he had been free from the chains of death, but over the past few months, there was a constant pull over his spirit that all was not what it was meant to be. Something lay beyond his reach. Something had not yet fully materialized. Malak had become silent on the subject, focusing his energy on teaching Jonathan to lead the fugitives to their freedom from the chains of death.

Life in Soteria was far better than anything he had ever known. He lived with family and friends in a beautiful valley filled with everything he needed, but with each new day, he found himself lonelier than the one before. Jonathan had once asked where the Bene Elohim had come from. Malak had only said that he came from a place far across the mountains that he did not truly understand. All would expose itself in due time; he would tell Jonathan. Even though he was free of the chains of death, everything in the Shadow Realm had to be conquered before the veil could be fully lifted, Malak would say. Jonathan's job was to continue to lead the fugitives to safety and prepare the army for a final battle. When? Jonathan would ask, but Malak did not know. When it is time, he would answer.

All those things mattered little to Jonathan now. He knew that he must be reunited with Lillian, no matter the costs. He had to save her and lead her to freedom. Malak had once promised him that, when the time was right, he would get the chance to save her, but that it would be Lillian's own desire that would lead her to freedom. All Jonathan could do was show her the way, but she had to come willingly.

So much had changed since the last time he had traveled this path. Before, he led a band of new friends to the promised safety of the river, the Sahat and knights of Kratos pursuing. Now he rode the same trail back toward the place where he had first found the Light with no fear of the darkness and with a full assurance that with the Light, he could not fail. But he also knew that the Shadow Realm still held evils that could ensnare him and could destroy his destiny, even though it no longer had the power to kill him. Malak had warned that he must continue to trust the Light because that was the only power that ultimately could overcome the Shadow Realm.

Jonathan knew that he would never fully understand what the Shadow Realm hid from him until the emptiness in his very being was filled, but what was that emptiness? How could he fill the void in his being unless he knew what it was that he needed to search for?

Suddenly his horse stopped, bringing Jonathan's thoughts back to the present and the task at hand. They had traveled several hours through the dark forest, and the horse had stopped at a place in the trail that led out from the forest into an open area covered in thick brush and young trees. A small stream flowed past them somewhere nearby in the darkness and to one side the rock wall of the canyon lay exposed and offered shelter.

"Okay girl, I guess we have ridden far enough for one night," Jonathan said.

The horse neighed and pawed her hooves in the soft dirt, agreeing with him and most likely saying as well that she had gone far enough for one night, Jonathan thought. He smiled, patted the horse and dismounted. Jonathan placed his gear next to the rock and unsaddled the horse, allowing her to graze on the lush grass by the stream. He then laid out his bedding under the overhang and gathered kindling to build a small fire. The Light glowed softly around him, soothing his worried spirit as he cooked a small meal and sat by the rock to eat. He then tethered the horse nearby and added more wood to the fire. Placing Patrick's sword next to him, he pulled the blanket over him as the night grew colder as a soft wind blew in from the north. Although he no longer feared the night, there were still many dangers in the Shadow Realm, and he always kept his weapon close to him.

Jonathan woke suddenly from a deep sleep with a vague memory of disturbing dreams that he could not remember. It was full daylight. Only gray ash remained of the fire from the night before, and his horse stood directly over him, staring down at him as if asking why Jonathan had slept so long and why she was still tethered.

The morning air was cold. Jonathan scattered the gray ashes out until he found a few red embers hiding beneath. He added a few handfuls of dry grass, and after blowing a few times, a new fire suddenly sprang up. He quickly added a few sticks and was rewarded with a bright fire that pushed away the morning chill. Jonathan untied the horse and led her to the stream and the grass and then knelt and drank from the crystal waters himself. With the daylight, Jonathan saw that he had camped next to a considerable mountain slope of young trees that had recently grown in after a forest fire had burned through the area.

Jonathan immediately recognized the place. The last time he had been here, he had been with Patrick, Peter, and Heather and they had narrowly escaped a wildfire intentionally set to attempt to trap them. Now the burned over mountainside was alive with new growth. What once had been a smoking, blackened mountain of death, now bloomed with a million wildflowers among a lush pine and hardwood forest of sapling size trees.

What a beautiful sight, Jonathan thought. Even when he had been a fugitive, he had always loved the forest. He felt safer within the majestic trees. Now he understood, that even though evil could kill and destroy, the Light could, given time, make all things bloom again. With the Light, life would always triumph over death, he reasoned.

Jonathan continued his journey across the mountain range until he finally reached a point high on the ridge where he could look over the Plains of Apistia. For as far as he could see, lay an endless prairie that led to the far Hills of Halom and the Crystalline Mountains. To the north, he could barely make out the vague outline of the walled city of Hedone. Closer in and toward the west, the rock Monuments of Life raised far above the grassland. The only way he knew to reach Halom was through the monuments. Hopefully this time around, he would have a better time of finding his way through the maze, he thought.

Jonathan knew that he would have to be very careful as he traveled past the city because as far as he knew, patrols still ranged the grasslands around the walls. The fugitive that had told him of Lillian's capture had also shown him a way into the Crystalline Mountains themselves, but he had to pass very close to the city of Hedone to find the trail. The last he had heard, the city closed the gates at night, so if he traveled past the town in the darkness, he should not have any problems. The inhabitants still feared the night. He did not, and he would use that to his advantage.

So, Jonathan did an unusual thing while traveling in the Shadow Realm. He stopped to wait out the day and would resume his travel at night. He found a perch on a rocky ledge where he could look over the grassland and see the city and sat to wait. He pulled his telescope from his pack and peered through the lens to get a closer look at the city.

Jonathan was very familiar with Hedone, having traveled there once a year for his entire life as required by law. Typically, the battlements were full of multicolored flags that seemed to always blow outward even when there was no wind. Archers always patrolled the walls, and the city gates would be open in the day. Travelers from all over the realm always came during the day to trade. Even the nomads would camp outside the walls as they waited to sell their herds to the city dwellers. The city was full of people who lived under the protection of Archon Sarkinos. Like the fugitives, they knew they were chained, but they decorated their chains with precious metals and jewels and lived their lives as if the chains had no power to finally kill them. But in the end, the chains always did. While a fugitive, Jonathan had always tried to find work in the city and live there, but only the rich could stay. Everyone else would be barred from the city at night.

He looked through the eyeglass but saw no flags on the walls. There were no guards, no nomad tents outside the walls. The city appeared to be empty, abandoned, decaying. Something wrong had happened, Jonathan reasoned. He studied the city for several minutes and concluded that the city had been abandoned. What had happened? What could have destroyed the largest city in the realm? Could it be? Could he have somehow destroyed Archon Sarkinos' power when he defeated Krino?

And then he saw the man standing above the city gate, and he knew with the sight of him that he looked at Archon Sarkinos himself. Jonathan stood up as if by standing, he would get a better view of the man and he knew instinctively that Archon Sarkinos could see him as well. Jonathan heard a voice call as if riding on the wind.

"I have been waiting for you," the voice said.

MACKENZIE'S JOURNAL
DAY THREE

But how does this help me in my time of need?
True faith believes that we truly are the habitation of an eternal God, that the Holy Spirit within us is above all and beyond all, therefore we are above all and beyond all.
TRUE FAITH IS.
I am that I am. My Kingdom is the person of Jesus living in the souls of mankind.

CHAPTER TWELVE

Jonathan stared in disbelief at what he had heard. He looked through the telescope again and saw the figure of a robed man standing on the battlements, staring directly at him.

"YOU MUST ACCEPT THE CHALLENGE"

Jonathan trusted the voice within him now. He placed the telescope back in its case and mounted the horse. Patrick's broadsword lay in its leather scabbard fastened to the horse's flanks. He held tightly to the hilt at first and then suddenly realized that the sword would probably not help him now. Slowly, Jonathan walked the horse down the steep slope to the grassland and lost sight of the city, but he knew in which direction to travel to reach the gates. The city was several miles away across the prairie and Jonathan spurred the horse to a fast trot down the wagon road, ever wary of a patrol that might lie in ambush. But, deep down, he knew that his suspicion was right. Something had happened, and Hedone lay abandoned, the walls crumbling. What power had caused that to happen?

After a shorter period then even Jonathan thought possible, the great city walls suddenly rose upward from behind the small hill that had hidden them from view. The great walls stretched out of sight in both directions. The great stone ramparts and battlements looked aged and broken, some sections wholly shattered and fallen in as if a vast army had besieged the walls with siege engines. The only sound was from a soft breeze that whistled eerily through the empty windows in the walls. Jonathan stopped a few dozen feet in front of the massive wooden gates that stood shut. He looked to where Sarkinos had stood, but there was no one standing above the entrance on the wall. What magic was this?

The horse stomped nervously and backed away from the wall, apprehensive of what lay behind. The horse snorted; her eyes panicky. Jonathan held tightly to the reins and calmed her.

"Easy now girl. It's okay," Jonathan softly spoke and patted her neck, leaning over and whispering, "It's okay girl. There is nothing to be afraid of."

Jonathan looked back up and for the first time, saw Sarkinos standing in front of the closed city gate. He was a tall man, handsome and well groomed. He wore long silk robes covered with jewelry and sandaled feet. Jonathan had seen the Archon many times, but never this close. The man wore makeup like a woman. He had short hair and bright blue eyes. Behind him stood two women, fully armored, each wearing a sword at their side and carrying a spear in one hand. They stood at total attention behind their leader.

The horse suddenly jumped and sidestepped, and Jonathan saw that two more warriors stood behind him. Where had they come from? He thought. Jonathan clasped the broadsword.

Sarkinos waved his hand, and the women moved away.

"No worries Jonathan, the great Apostolos Or. I mean you no harm. You are welcome here at the great city of Hedone. May you come inside and dine with me?"

Jonathan eyed the man, trying to calculate his true motives. He then looked up and down the walls again, seeing the great damage that had been done to the mighty walls, now crumbling even more as he stood watching them.

"I don't see a great city. I see a crumbling mess," Jonathan teased.

Sarkinos appeared not to have been affected by the comment, "Just a temporary setback Jonathan. Rest assured; you will be back among us again. In time, the pleasures of life will overtake you, and you will fill this city once again. I was waiting for you to arrive and here you are. Now come in and dine with me. You must be hungry from your travels."

"I have not come to see you, Sarkinos. I have other places to be."

"Oh, I know, I know. You search for the girl. But that will be your downfall, boy. She will not take you back, you know. She blames you for all that has happened. It is a trap, I tell you. A trap. But I offer a better way. My way is pleasure. Join me, and I will help you get the girl back, on your terms, not hers."

"How do you know about the girl?" Jonathan asked.

"No matter. I have great power in this land. I know all that goes on even in the realms of the others of my kind," Sarkinos answered.

"Your power must be weak, Sarkinos, for your great city to have been attacked and destroyed."

Sarkinos laughed," Jonathan, you try to upset me. You think you know, but you know nothing. Like I said before, what you see is only a temporary thing. You will again fill the city with your presence. You think the old ways have been destroyed when your chains were removed, but you are wrong. The pleasures of life will overcome even the strongest among you, given time."

Jonathan wanted to turn the horse around and run away. Not because he feared the Archon, but that he somehow knew that a portion of what the man said could be true. What kept him there was the fact that the voice had told him to accept the challenge and he knew that he had to trust the Light and lean not on his understanding. He knew that somehow, he had to overcome whatever lay before him before he could travel on to find Lillian.

Sarkinos motioned with his hand, and the women disappeared behind a small door beside the gate. A great section of the wall suddenly gave way and crashed outward across the grassland, spooking the horse. Jonathan calmed the mare as Sarkinos waited patiently for the gate to open, totally disregarding what had just happened. The Archon was delusional, Jonathan thought.

"Now, once again, I offer safe passage through Hedone. Please come and dine with me, Jonathan and then you can freely leave to find the girl if you wish." Sarkinos asked again as the gate fully opened, revealing the city within the walls.

Ruins, Jonathan thought. The whole city appeared to lie in ruins. Sarkinos walked through the gates and stood to one side, waving Jonathan through the opening. Jonathan hesitated. This could be a trap, he thought.

"IT IS."

Then why do I go in? Jonathan asked himself. There was no answer, but Jonathan knew that he would have to enter the city and confront whatever lay inside. He would have to accept the challenge; the voice had told him. That only meant that he had the strength to overcome already within him, he thought.

"YOU DO."

The horse suddenly shied away from the opening. The mare had no desire to enter the gates. Jonathan spurred her forward, but she only sidestepped across the gateway. She snorted, pulling her head back and flared her nostrils, her eyes wild with fear and Jonathan lowered his head, patting her neck, "It's okay girl."

Jonathan looked carefully through the opening into the city streets beyond the door. What had spooked the horse? The roads themselves were full of wagons, furniture and turned over carts. Gold, silver, and jewels of all kinds sparkled in the sunshine; piles of treasure scattered all across the courtyard as if an invading army had looted the treasure houses but failed to carry the wealth with them as they left.

The horse calmed and walked into the courtyard but appeared to be nervous. Something about the place scared the mare. There had been fires throughout the city it seemed because Jonathan could see the charred remains of dozens of buildings down the courtyard where the city market had once held thousands of merchants. What could have caused all of this? What army was strong enough to destroy the great city of Hedone?

"Please excuse the mess, but this is all temporary, you will see. Please dismount your horse. The horse will be fine, I promise, and come in and dine with me," Sarkinos invited.

Jonathan sat for a moment on the horse. He did not want to dismount. In fact, he wished to ride from this place as fast as the mare would carry him, but he felt a strong reassurance that he was going to be okay. He instinctively felt for the Light that hung from the leather cord around his neck and was rewarded with its warm vibration. He glanced down at his hand. The Light glowed brightly within the hand that covered it.

Jonathan suddenly dismounted and disconnected the scabbard and sword from the saddle and slung the weapon over his shoulder the way Patrick had taught him to do as Sarkinos watched.

Sarkinios chuckled, "You don't need that here, Jonathan, you are the Apostolos Or, are you not?"

Jonathan ignored the Archon and led the mare to a hitching post and tied her there with a slip knot that she could release if he whistled for her very quickly. He reached into the pack and retrieved an apple and held the fruit up to her nose. She promptly grabbed the apple and ate it as Jonathan petted her and reassured her that everything was fine. The noise of the horse chewing the apple was overly loud because of the extreme silence all around him. Where were all the people?

MACKENZIE'S JOURNAL
DAY FOUR

If we truly allow God to build a habitation in His holy temple, which is us, then the Kingdom of God will yield all that it needs to sustain our earthly lives. The rain will come, the wind will blow, the sun will shine, the storms will rage, the garden will flourish, the fruit will ripen, the love will flow, and the flowers will bloom.

All mankind will see the Kingdom of God in you.

CHAPTER THIRTEEN

With one more reassuring pat, Jonathan turned to face Sarkinos who stood by an open door. Jonathan followed Sarkinos through the door and down a short hallway that led to an enormous banquet hall. Jonathan stopped at the door to the room, amazed at the sight before him.

The room stretched over a hundred feet to the far wall where a tremendously large, stone fireplace dominated the wall. A massive fire roared within the fireplace. Both side walls were covered with beautiful tapestries that hung from the cathedral ceiling down to the marble floor. The tapestries showed all types of wildlife walking among a garden of beautiful trees bearing multicolored fruit. Majestic, snow-capped mountains rose in the background. Trees of all species and shapes dotted the landscape interspersed with open meadows filled with flowers. Jonathan's first impression was that he had walked into the most beautiful garden he had ever seen.

Down the center of the room stood an oak banquet table that appeared to have been cut from a single tree, a tree more massive than anything Jonathan had ever seen in all the forests he had ever traveled through. High backed, oak chairs lined each side of the massive table, the chairs ornately carved with the shapes of animals of all types. Three large, crystal chandeliers hung on golden chains above the banquet table. Swinging from the chandeliers were birds crafted from multicolored jewels as if they were flying. The sun's light shone through high windows in the ceiling and created sparkling prism lights through the dancing birds.

The table was set for two people. To one side a buffet was covered with all types of food, and two servants stood silently by the door leading out to a kitchen off to one side of the banquet hall. When Sarkinos entered the room, both servants bowed, keeping their heads down. Jonathan looked around for the warrior women, but they were not in the room, which immediately worried him. Where had they gone?

Sarkinos pulled back the closer chair and sat down, motioning for Jonathan to set in the chair across the table from him. They both set at the very end of the table across the room from the fireplace on the opposite end of the banquet hall. Sarkinos then clapped his hands once, and the servant girls immediately rushed to place all the food on the table between the two. They filled their glasses with red wine and sparkling water and then hurriedly left the room.

Sarkinos tasted the wine and smiled approvingly, "There Jonathan, please try the wine. It's the best that you will find in the entire realm."

Jonathan only set there staring at Sarkinos. The food smelled incredible, and he was hungry, but did he dare eat or drink?

"Oh, my friend. I assure you the food and drink will not hurt you. If I had wanted to kill you, I could have done so already." Sarkinos stated.

No, you could not, Jonathan thought as he continued to stare at the Archon as he drank from the goblet.

"Oh well, suit yourself, but I am famished," Sarkinos remarked as he stabbed a thick chunk of beef from the dish before him. "But at least enjoy the music while I eat."

Sarkinos clapped his hands twice and immediately a harp began playing from somewhere in the room, the beautiful chords echoing off the ceiling. Jonathan looked and saw a woman in a flowing white gown playing a large, golden harp by the fireplace. The harp music was very soothing, Jonathan thought, and the food smelled incredible. He was hungry, but could he trust the food not to harm him?

Sarkinos finished the first cut of beef and stabbed another along with potatoes and vegetables from the second tray as Jonathan continued to watch, wondering what the Archon was thinking. What trap did he have planned?

"This is delicious. Don't be a fool, Jonathan, eat with me and we will talk. There is much that I would like to show you."

Jonathan finally gave in and pulled a bit of the beef from the same cut that Sarkinos had taken a portion from. He then added a few potatoes and began to eat. The food was the best that he had ever tasted. Sarkinos stopped eating for a moment and smiled.

"Its good, very good. I knew you would enjoy the food. The best cooks in all the land are right here in Hedone." Sarkinos remarked.

Jonathan took a drink of water and wiped the beef drippings from his mouth and chin with the cloth napkin. He set the napkin down and looked directly at Sarkinos who set there smiling at him.

"You said you were waiting for me. Why?" Jonathan asked.

"Yes, yes. Right to the point I see. Of course, you are. You are the great Apostolos Or. Quite the different man than when you used to come each year to these very gates, begging for entrance to my city so a link of chains could be removed. Now you come as a great conqueror after destroying the very thing that you always cherished."

Jonathan was confused by what the Archon had said, "What do you mean that I destroyed the city? I did not know the city had been destroyed until this very day."

Jonathan pushed himself away from the table, "And I never cherished this place. I came each year because it was the law. I begged to stay each time because it was better than a life starving in the wilderness, but each time, I was kicked out until another year passed."

Sarkinos disregarded the second question, but answered the first, "I was waiting for you because I knew you would return. You have always returned in the past. You have always lived among us, Jonathan. Hedone is all about the pleasures of life. You were born here. You were raised in this place. Each time you think you have destroyed this city; you always come back and rebuild it. The city is full of riches, pleasures of life, everything that you need to take all the pain of living away. "

Jonathan stared at the Archon incredulous, not believing what he was saying. How could any of this be? He had never lived in Hedone. He only visited it each year to take a link of chains away as was the law. That had been before the Light had wholly removed the chains. But he had never partaken of the pleasures of the city. The city had never allowed him to stay long enough to do so.

"Oh, now Jonathan, I see that you are confused. Think a minute. Each year you came to remove a link to the chain, but you stayed many a time. You did enjoy all that this city had to offer. You have always lived among us, enjoying all that the city is. But now that you have the magic of the Light, you can live here like an Archon. Hedone was only temporary. Now what you see around you can be forever."

Suddenly the tapestries along the walls grew outward, and the room began to transform. A wind blew through the room, and the jeweled birds became real. The tapestry animals materialized into real animals, and Jonathan stood in a beautiful garden, Sarkinos beside him.

They were both standing on a hill overlooking a city that was rebuilding itself before them. The crumbling walls of Hedone were growing level by level. Towers rose upward from the rubble. People materialized out of the ground and began to populate the city once more. Jonathan was astonished at what he was seeing. So beautiful, he thought.

"See Jonathan. The Light's magic has given you such power to rebuild the crumbling walls. You can live like an Archon, ruler of the city. All you see can be yours."

Jonathan could remember all the times that he had tried to remain in the city, but each time he had been thrown out. Could this be true? Could he now be the ruler of the city? Is that the true power of the Light, to live in this beautiful garden and rule over the city of life's pleasures?

And then, he felt an intense heat burning into his heart, and he looked away from the scene before him and down to the Light around his neck.

"THE LIGHT IS NOT MAGIC JONATHAN. THE LIGHT IS TRUTH."

Jonathan drew his sword from the sheath and turned to face Sarkinos but found himself sitting in the chair in the banquet hall, and the sword still hung over his shoulder. Sarkinos sat across from him, drinking from the goblet.

"Oh well. I tried. You seek the harder path," Sarkinos said and snapped his fingers.

A dark figure jumped out from behind the tapestry and Jonathan pushed back from the table and rolled over just as a spear shaft embedded itself in the chair back. Jonathan scrambled back, drew his sword and whistled loudly, just in time to parry the flashing sword. Another warrior jumped across the table, spear in hand as Sarkinos quickly exited the banquet hall.

Jonathan pulled out another chair and threw it under the first woman, who tried to jump over it, but become entangled in the legs and fell forward. Jonathan slashed forward with his sword and drew blood. The woman screamed in both anger and pain, and suddenly two more warriors were in the room and Jonathan was surrounded. Jonathan parried another blow and pulled down a tapestry just as his horse charged through the door and knocked a warrior from the table. The torn tapestry floated downward, covering the other two and Jonathan mounted the mare and rode past the struggling warriors out the door into the courtyard.

The walls were crashing down all around him, and the only way out of the ruined city was through the wooden gate that was slowly swinging shut. The horse turned on her own accord and raced toward the door as it closed further, barely making it out of the city before the massive gate slammed shut.

Jonathan reined in the horse and turned. Before him, the great walled city of Hedone crumbled in mighty explosions of rock and dirt. The ground under him shook from the power of the city walls as they fell.

Jonathan did not fully understand all that had just happened. He did not realize what Sarkinos had told him. But somehow, he knew that a part of him had been in the city. That somehow in the past, maybe he had partially or even completely destroyed the city, only to rebuild it again, just as it seemed he was about to do again just moments before.

Malak had once said that the Shadow Realm was not the truth and that the true kingdom lay elsewhere and there was much about the realm that he would only understand when the true kingdom was revealed. As he stood there watching the great city turn into a pile of rubble, he thought that he would have just to accept what had happened as is and that one day he would understand, but this was not the day.

He turned to leave, but suddenly reined in the mare and turned back to face the rubble. Standing in the middle of the fallen city was Sarkinos.

"I will be waiting for you, Jonathan. When you return, I will still be here. This is only temporary. One day, you will see." he shouted from across the barren landscape.

Jonathan did not answer him. He turned away, just as he had done to Krino by the river. Sarkinos was no longer relevant in his life. He knew the way to Lillian now. That was all that mattered.

MACKENZIE'S JOURNAL
DAY FIVE

How it is God that I can walk in the garden with you, yet the garden is my soul?

The wonders of God are unfathomable even while experiencing the Kingdom in all its glory.

CHAPTER FOURTEEN

Once more, the knock on the door woke Lillian up in her bedroom. The servant girl opened the door and quietly scurried past the bed to open the curtains, revealing another glorious sunrise. A soft, warm, flower-scented breeze blew in with the open window. A flock of birds fluttered noisily just outside the window. One sparrow flew into the room, flapping around the ceiling.

"Good morning Gloria," Lillian said as she stretched and yawned. She had slept better the previous night then during the last week that she had been here. No strange dreams or bad memories haunted her sleep like before.

"Good morning mistress Lillian," the girl answered as she quickly took a broom and swatted at the small bird, driving it back out the window. "Your breakfast is ready."

"Wonderful, I will be right down. Will you eat with me this morning?" Lillian asked.

The servant girl only smiled, bowed and exited the door, not to be seen again until before dinner. Lillian had tried to talk with the girl, but she had only said her name. Lillian dressed and quickly made her way through the now familiar corridors to the veranda in the courtyard behind the stone structure where, like before, the table was set for three and two servants stood quietly by a buffet full of breakfast food including meats, cheeses, bread, eggs, and fruits.

Lillian set down at the table and looked up to see Zanah sitting across the table from her. The woman wore her riding outfit along with her armor and sword. Lillian thought it strange that she was there in that attire.

"Good morning dear. I hope you slept well," Zanah said.

"Yes, I did, thank you," Lillian answered as the servants filled their plates with the food.

Zanah waved the servants away, not wishing to eat anything. They quickly packed up the food and left.

"Have you enjoyed your stay here?" Zanah asked.

Between bites, Lillian answered her, "Yes. This place is amazing. I'm so thankful to you for allowing me to stay in your home this week. I could live here forever."

Zanah smiled. Her magic had finally taken full control over the girl. She appeared not to have remembered anything of her past. To Lillian, she had been in the valley for only a week, but Zanah knew that she had been here for over three months. Much had changed outside the valley that Lillian had no idea of, but in the valley, the girl wasted her days away blissfully exploring the valley like a child in a playground.

But Zanah knew that she would have to remind the girl of one crucial fact so the plan could become a reality.

"Lillian, do you remember why I brought you here?"

Lillian looked at Zanah, questioning, and had to think for a moment. Vague memories flooded her mind, memories of riding horses, fires, large tents trampled by charging demons on horseback, her dreams from days before. But nothing substantial came to mind that could answer the question. Why was she here? It seemed like this world was the only world that she had ever known. But that could not be true, Lillian thought. She had only been here a week, or had she?

"It's okay child. You have been through a lot, and this place does a wonderful job of replacing unwanted memories with pleasant ones. However, I need you to remember one thing about why you are here," Zanah continued as she stared intently at the girl, weaving a spell over her mind that would only draw out the solid memories that Zanah wished for the girl to know.

Lillian thought hard about the question, and suddenly a man appeared in her thoughts. Who was he? Lillian saw him standing before her, reaching outward toward her, a shining object in his hands. She remembered then. His name was Jonathan, and she had loved him. She still loved him and missed him terribly.

Zanah fought hard to push past the memory and distort it, but true love was very hard to overcome, but she finally did.

And then Lillian suddenly remembered why she had been brought to the valley. Jonathan had betrayed them by bringing the Light among them. He had brought the Bene Elohim into her clan, and they had killed her family. She was here to take the Light from him so that it could be destroyed once and for all.

Zanah smiled at her handiwork. Deception was such a potent tool against the Light, she thought.

"I do remember. When Jonathan gives me the Light, I am to take it from him and give it to you. The Light will then be destroyed forever," Lillian exclaimed.

"Yes, very good. He should be here sometime within the next few days. All you must do is continue to enjoy your time in this place. Go anywhere in the valley you wish, ride the horses if you like. Sometime, he will find you. Don't worry, he won't hurt you, but he will try to convince you that you are a prisoner here, that the Light is the only way to freedom. You must make him believe that you truly believe in what he is saying. If he believes you, he will give you the Light. Don't worry child. Remember, you overcame its magic once before, you can again. When he gives the Light to you, you must run away as fast as you can. Do everything in your power to escape him. I will be close by. Once you have the Light, Jonathan's power will be no more. When you escape, you must give the Light to me, and I will destroy it. Do you understand?"

"Yes, my Lady," Lillian answered.

Zanah smiled, "Good child. Now don't worry about anything. Go out, enjoy the garden. There are horses in the corral. You love horses, right?" Lillian nodded. "Well go and ride any you wish. Do whatever you want until Jonathan finds you."

The spell worked perfectly, Zanah thought.

"Yes, my Lady," Lillian answered, but Zanah was no longer sitting in the chair. Lillian sat alone as if no one had ever been there.

MACKENZIE'S JOURNAL
DAY SIX

Nothing is as it appears in our world. Things change. Grow dim as night approaches, sleeps in dark places, moves from shadow to shadow, from light to light, shifting from place to place. Uncertainty. Fear. Strife. The poverty of man's soul. Sleeplessness. Doubts. Fear. Concern. Emptiness. Jealousy. Fear again and again and again…..

The garden becomes polluted so easily if the gates are left open, and the gardener is forced away. But if the gardener is present and the gates are shut, allowing only love and fellowship in, then there is only the rain, the sunshine, a gentle breeze, a violent storm that comes in wonder and power and LIFE.

No shadows, no darkness, no doubt. Only love, only oneness with God, true fellowship with God, true love from God. And the flowers bloom, the trees grow, fruits of all types erupt, and entire nations are fed.

Seek the wisdom of God. He will tell you what to do in all things and all circumstances. Just follow His counsel in the matters of life in this earthly existence. Then the reality of living now in the eternity of today in the garden of God is the true reality, is the journey of grace, a journey of pure fun, adventure, love, fellowship. The glory of God shines forth through all the realities of man, the shadows created by mankind.

CHAPTER FIFTHTEEN

A knock on the bedroom door woke Lillian up. She had slept better than any of the other nights for the past week she had been in the home with no bad dreams to haunt her night.

"Good morning, mistress. Your breakfast is ready," Gloria said as she pulled back the curtains and opened the windows.

Bright morning sun shone through the window, bringing with it the amazing smell of the beautiful garden outside. Lillian set up in bed and stretched, watching as the young, servant girl picked up Lillian's clothing she had worn the day before. They were filthy and covered in mud. That was strange, Lillian thought.

"I will clean these Mistress. You have fresh clothing on the bed," the girl said and scurried back to the door.

"Gloria," Lillian exclaimed, and the girl turned at the door, "Please eat with me this morning."

Gloria smiled and bowed, "I cannot mistress, but you enjoy your day," she said and shut the door behind her.

Lillian dressed and walked to the door and out onto the balcony that overlooked the garden below. The valley stretched out to the far cliffs, covered in trees and meadows, streams and waterfalls. Such a beautiful sight, Lillian thought. She could live here forever. But she remembered that there was one thing that she had to do. Someone would come for her, and she was to take something from him and give it to Zanah. She thought for a moment but could not remember anything else.

Lillian heard the faint sound of harp music playing below and whispered voices from the graveled trails in the garden, but looking carefully, she could see no one. Birds flew past her out over the trees toward the cliffs, and for just a moment, Lillian thought she saw blue mountains beyond the Crystalline Cliffs. But that could not be, she thought. Nothing existed past the cliffs, only emptiness where no man could go. She stared at the location and again saw a blue mountain range through a gap in the fog. The slopes were covered with trees. Below the mountains, a walled city stood, the gates glistening like gold in the sunlight. Thin columns of white smoke rose peacefully upward from multiple chimneys along the walls. She thought that she could hear the faint echoing of bells ringing. What place was this?

And suddenly, she felt an extreme pain within her side as if something had been torn from her. She doubled over, almost falling to the floor before catching herself by the railing. The pain quickly subsided, leaving a deep throbbing in her side and a feeling of total emptiness as if she was only half a person. What a strange thought? She stood up and looked again to the cliffs and saw the mountain range still there, beyond the cliffs where no land was supposed to be. What magic was this?

"THIS IS ALL AN ILLUSION. THIS DOMAIN WAS NEVER MEANT TO BE. THE TRUE KINGDOM IS OUT THERE."

Lillian stepped back, shocked. There had been a voice somewhere. She looked around, but there was no one there. But she had heard a voice calling from somewhere far off, yet very close. She suddenly thought of Jonathan, of how she loved him, missed him something terrible. Where was he? Was he the person coming for her?

She was startled by a knock at the door and turned quickly.

"Good morning, mistress. Your breakfast is ready," Gloria said.

Lillian set up in bed and stretched, watching as the young, servant girl picked up Lillian's clothing she had worn the day before. They were filthy and covered in mud. That was strange, Lillian thought.

"I will clean these Mistress. You have fresh clothing on the bed," the girl said and scurried back to the door.

"Gloria," Lillian exclaimed, and the girl turned at the door, "Please eat with me this morning."

Gloria smiled and bowed, "I cannot mistress, but you enjoy your day," she said and shut the door behind her.

Lillian stood up to dress, totally confused about what had just happened. She had been at the window, had she not? She shook her head. Something was not what it appeared to be.

Lillian walked through the familiar hallways out to the veranda as she had done for the past few days, or was it longer? As customary, the two servants stood by the buffet full of food, and the table was set for three people. Lillian smiled at the two servants who bowed respectfully. She set down at the chair. The servants immediately filled her plate with food and left, leaving her alone to eat.

Usually, Lillian was always famished, but this morning she was not hungry at all. The happenings in her room earlier had unsettled her, and she could not eat, but just played with her food with the fork. The haunting voice troubled her. What did it mean? The true kingdom was out there, it had said. Did it refer to the city beyond the cliffs she had seen?

"Are you not hungry child?" Zanah asked from her seat across the table.

Lillian jumped and dropped the fork.

Zanah was surprised at her reaction, "Are you okay, Lillian?" she asked.

Lillian composed herself and retrieved the fork, "Yes, you just startled me, that's all. I didn't see you come in."

Zanah studied her closely, looking deep into her mind to ensure that the spell was still intact. It seemed to be okay, she thought.

Zanah smiled, "What have you planned to do today?" she asked.

"I think I will ride over to the waterfalls today. I have only seen them from the balcony and would love to see them closer. Is that okay?" Lillian answered. For some reason, she thought it better that she not ask about what she had seen earlier.

Zanah studied her intently before answering. Something was not quite right with the girl, but the spell seemed to be working fine, so she agreed, "That's fine. Do be careful though. And I may join you later. I have not been to the falls for some time myself."

Lillian nodded and managed to eat a bit of the food. She wanted to get a closer look at the mountain range and hoped that Zanah would not join her.

Zanah stared into Lillian's mind. There seemed to still be a residue of the Light somewhere, but she could not find the source, "Lillian do you remember why I have brought you to this place?"

Lillian remembered everything, "Yes my lady. I am to make Jonathan believe that I wish for him to give me the Light and when he does, I am to run away and give the Light to you."

Lillian also remembered her feelings for Jonathan, "But I am worried about Jonathan. You will not hurt him, will you?"

So that was it, Zanah thought. The girl still loved Jonathan. She smiled. Love was an intense emotion, she knew. One that her spells would have trouble dealing with. In fact, she knew that love in contact with the Light became more than just an emotion. Love became a part of the Light itself. In fact, she knew that the Light was Love. But she did not worry. In Lillian's case, she could use the emotion to her advantage.

"No child. Of course not. I only wish to destroy the Light itself. Jonathan is trapped by its evil. By destroying the Light, you can free Jonathan, and the two of you can live in my garden forever."

Lillian nodded, "Thank you, my Lady."

And Lillian found herself once more in the empty veranda all alone.

MACKENZIE'S JOURNAL
DAY SEVEN

I arise this morning. The first thing I think about is you. When you sleep, I am there. As you go about your day, I am there. No matter if you believe in me or not, I am always with you. I dream of a time when you and I can become as one, just as the Father and I are one.

Sleep in peace. Even when you are awake, your spirit can rest in me in peace. Your soul is the place where my spirit was meant to live. You were created to be a temple for me to live, a dwelling place, and a land where you and I can walk in the coolness of the morning. The way it was meant to be, the way it was from the beginning of man's existence.

CHAPTER SIXTEEN

Lillian sat in the chair for a few minutes, trying to understand what had happened to her this morning, but could not. But she knew that somehow, she needed to find out once and for all what lay beyond the cliffs and where the voice had come from. Zanah had said that Jonathan was close, and when he came, she would take the Light from him and give it to Zanah as she had promised, but she needed to figure out what strange things were going on around her. Also, for some reason since hearing the voice, she did not trust everything Zanah had told her. Lillian would have to be careful; she thought and did not know why she felt that. But she felt the emptiness inside her and remembered that she had felt that feeling before, ever since seeing the strange apparition behind Jonathan the last time she had seen him. All was not what it appeared to be, she thought.

Lillian left the veranda and walked around the back of the stone house to the barns where several horses grazed in the corral. She had ridden each of the horses in the corral but preferred the big black and white and called him over. She had named him Traveler.

Lillian led Traveler into the barn, where she quickly saddled him and mounting up, she rode out the gate and across the meadow. She spooked a herd of deer and reined in the horse to set and watch them bound away across the meadow. Everything about the valley was peaceful, she thought. Such beauty, peace, and joy everywhere she looked.

As she set on the horse and watched the deer, she remembered something the voice had said before, but could not remember when or in what circumstance. Three words came to mind when she thought of the kingdom behind the cliffs.

"VIRTUE, PEACE, JOY," the voice had spoken.

She felt peace and joy in this garden, she thought, but for the first time, she realized that for some reason she thought that virtue was somehow missing. What a strange thought. Virtue meant righteous, purity, clean, wholesome, but somehow deep under the surface of all around her, she suddenly felt the total opposite of all these things. Why was she thinking such crazy thoughts, she asked herself?

The deer bounded away into the trees, and Lillian spurred Traveler onward toward the far side of the valley. She crossed a rushing river that rose above her knees and then dismounted and took a drink from the refreshing waters as Traveler stood nearby. A bear suddenly appeared from the brush nearby, but she was not alarmed. In this place, she had learned that the animals were harmless. The bear's presence did not spook even the horse. Lillian mounted the horse and continued. The fog continued to hide most of the mountain cliffs, but between the gap, Lillian could see the mountain range beyond very clearly.

Meanwhile Zanah had posted several guards across the entrance to the valley that the spy had told Jonathan was the only way in. They were to follow him until he found the girl and then attack when she took the Light from him. Satisfied with the preparation, she mounted her horse and turned just in time to see Lillian stop at the river to drink. She had planned to ride back to where Archon Planos was inspecting the army but thought that she better see what the girl was up to, especially because of how strangely she had acted at breakfast.

The entire time since Lillian had arrived, Zanah had been busy creating the soldiers to fill the ranks. As the Shadow Realm appeared to be shrinking, Planos had ordered the army built, and they planned to attack Soteria whether or not they had captured Jonathan.

Lillian continued across the meadow until she finally reached the base of the mountains. From this point, she could only see the ragged cliff walls that stretched upward into the foreboding fog above. But she knew that just above her, there was a gap in the wall and a city of gold behind it. She dismounted the horse and stared upward. There appeared to be no place where she could climb at this point to reach the gap.

She mounted Traveler again and rode away from the cliff walls to a point in the valley where she could see through the gap again. She sat there on the horse, transfixed by the sight above her. She was close enough now to see the mountains for what they were. From a distance, they appeared a blue haze, but closer; she could see the individual trees in full bloom even better than from the balcony. Meadows dotted the hillsides, and upon closer inspection, she noticed movement in the meadows. Something alive lived there and moved among the lush grass. Eagles soared in the heavens above, and suddenly one of them appeared to fly outward from the mountain range and flew high over her head on this side of the cliff walls, before reentering the other side and disappearing behind the fog.

Zanah stopped some distance behind her and was astonished at the sight of what the girl was staring at. How could this be, she thought? How could the girl have the power to see past the fog and into the Kingdom? No one in the Shadow Realm had ever been able to do so before. Somehow the barriers between kingdoms were crumbling. Zanah begin to chant her spell and taking her hand, she waved across the gap, and very slowly the fog increased, and her magic concealed the hole in the fog.

Lillian continued to look at the glorious image, hoping that she would hear the voice once more and then realized with sadness that the fog increased and slowly the image disappeared until only the cliff walls remained. Had she seen what she thought she had seen? There is no way that the image could be right?

"BUT IT IS TRUE. SOON ALL WILL BE REVEALED."

Lillian clearly heard the voice just before Traveler jumped in fear and turned suddenly, almost throwing her.

"Whoa boy!" Lillian gained control and looked once more at the cliff, but there was nothing there. But she knew now what she must do when Jonathan came.

Lillian turned and saw Zanah riding up.

Zanah was overly tired because of the strong magic that she had to use to cover the gap. It was much harder than before, she thought with alarm.

"I'm glad I caught you," she exclaimed, "What were you looking at?'

Lillian did not want to a tell her the total truth, "I thought I saw a mountain range across the cliffs, but that couldn't be. There is nothing beyond the cliffs but darkness. The fog swirls, and from a distance, I could see blue mountains, but I was wrong."

Zanah nodded," Yea I have thought that myself sometimes."

Zanah turned the horse back toward the stone house far across the valley, "We best be on our way back. Planos will join us for dinner tonight. We have much to talk about. Hopefully, Jonathan will come soon, and we can free him from the magic."

Lillian agreed and followed her back to the house, thinking that somehow the woman was losing herself in her lies. Lillian somehow now knew that all was not what it appeared to be, but she still did not know what it was supposed to be. All she understood was that she now knew what she would do when Jonathan came.

It was almost dark when the two women finally arrived at the veranda for dinner. Gloria stood by the door as always, and the two nameless servants stood by the buffet. The table had been set for three, but Planos was not there. Zanah appeared to be upset. Something bothered her more than Lillian had ever seen her be. Something had changed somewhat, and the servants knew not to test her. They feared her and stood silently while she paced back and forth, waiting for her counterpart to appear, but he never did. Finally, she excused herself from the veranda and left. This was fine by Lillian, who was very hungry and enjoyed the meal alone before retiring to her bedroom. She did notice, however, that there were two guards stationed at every door to the house, including her own.

MACKENZIE'S JOURNAL
DAY EIGHT

God bless this home, this life, this family…..
That prayer was answered even before you wrote the words. All is needed is for you to walk the journey day by day, for today is your eternity. If you are in me and I am in you, then each day is a blessed eternity onto itself.

The shadows wonder through the night. They even wonder through the light of day. But your steps are lighted by my hand. You only control the present time. That is all humanity is allotted to control. However, if you truly understand that you live a life of existence outside of time with me when you allow my Spirit to reside in the temple of your soul, then you will understand that by controlling your life in the present, you are controlling your life through all eternity.

You control this life of eternity by understanding that you are allowing me to control the life for you. This is true freedom.

All the responsibility for the outcome is upon my shoulders. You only have to live the life, enjoy the journey, rest in my grace, and flow through my spirit.

Time controls my children, but I did not even wish for that to happen. I created time the same way I created all things. You are my greatest creation. Originally you functioned outside of time, but now you have been placed within its constraints. But in me, you are above its control. You may live within its boundaries but think about it. Time helps you to exist in this natural world. It protects you, assists you, strengthens you, but you must master time.

Remember that you are a new creation, seated at the right hand of my son, above all things. Don't let time control you in a bad way. Use it as the gift that it was meant to be. A gift was given to all men in my creation. Use it to live your life in abundance. Value time, control it. Do not waste time and never let it control you. Remember that in the true reality, your soul is above it.

A man believes that when he passes from this life in mortal death, he passes into eternity. But the true reality is that when you are in me, and I am in you, you are already living in eternity. The Kingdom of God resides in your soul. The Kingdom of God, my Kingdom is the person of my son, Jesus.

Jesus crucified the constraints of time like everything else on the cross. Although it appears that you are bound by time, and in your present physical body you are, but the true reality is that you are even now an eternal being.

CHAPTER SEVENTEEN

Jonathan had ridden across the Plains of Apistia for only a day from the fallen city of Hedone, so he was shocked when on the second morning; he caught sight of the tree-lined river that marked the boundary of Halom. The last time he had been here, he had traveled for weeks across the plains with the nomads. It seemed as if the Shadow Realm was growing smaller, he thought. But how could that be?

He reined in the mare just behind a small rise above the river crossing. Jonathan dismounted and then pulled down on the mare, forcing her to lie down in the tall grass. He then crawled up to the hilltop so he could watch the crossing closely without being seen himself. What he saw before him both shocked and terrified him.

The river crossing itself looked just as he had remembered it. The nomad wagon trail ran into the water at the shallow area and then exited the far side. The corrals had been rebuilt since the attack, but he could still see burned out areas where individual wagons had burned. He thought of Lillian and how he could have tried to save her, but the crowd had pulled her away. And Malak had told he him to save Heather and flee. He knew now that the decision to do so was the only chance that he had, but it did not make him feel any better. He still thought that somehow, he had abandoned her.

But everything else about the crossing and the far side of the river had changed entirely. Where before only nomad tents had been visible, now walled fortresses covered the low hills from the river back toward the Crystalline Cliffs. And even more disturbing was the fact the cliffs themselves were no longer several days journey from the crossing but were now in some places immediately adjacent to the river itself. How could that be? What magic was this to cause the landscape itself to suddenly shrink in on itself?

But as shocking as the sight was to him, what terrified him was the thousands upon thousands of armored warriors who stood in solid ranks, line by line, across the plains between the river and the cliffs. A vast army assembled, complete with cavalry and siege engines. Horsemen stood to face each rank of soldiers and walked up and down the lines, inspecting the troops as they all stood still.

Where had all the soldiers come from? Jonathan lowered his head below the grass, astonished at what he had seen. He had to get word to Peter. How could the Soterians defend the crossing against such an army as this one? But how could he get word to them in time? It had taken him five days to get from Soteria to the crossing, Such a large army would take longer, but Peter would only have at most ten days to prepare for an assault, and that was if he knew about the army now. Jonathan knew that he would only have one chance to save Lillian and then they would have to ride as fast as they could back to warn Peter of what was coming.

Jonathan grabbed the Light tightly, fear for his friends welling inside. The Light warmed his hands and body as its power covered him, and he knew that he would have to entirely trust the Light, even though he did not understand all that was going on. Jonathan rose back up just above the grass and peered down into the valley below again. The ranks dismissed one by one, and the soldiers appeared to be going back to their camps. Jonathan breathed a big sigh of relief when he saw that they seemed not to be traveling today, so hopefully, there would be more time. Also, as he reflected on the developments, he knew that Peter was a trained soldier who had been preparing the defenses of Soteria for months now. When the army appeared, he would be ready, and Jonathan would be at his side with Lillian as well.

But now he had to rescue her. He had seen her while in the monuments and knew how to get to her. The experience in the monuments had confounded him, but with each day, he knew that the Shadow Realm was ever changing, and realms crossed that he had never known existed. He had somehow landed in a world where the Light was all around him and in all things. He had met the guard by the wall that had shown him a world that he said was a glimpse of the true kingdom, but that even that world was not the True Kingdom. And then he had given him the journal, which Jonathan had tried to read, but it made no sense to him as of yet. But he had also seen a way into the valley where Lillian was held captive, and it was not the way that the fugitive had told him about.

The more he thought about the story the fugitive had told him, the more he believed that it was a trap set for him. But that did not matter now. He knew where Lillian was and he knew how to get to her, and that was all he cared about.

Jonathan crawled back to where the mare lay, patiently waiting for him to return. "Good girl," Jonathan whispered and patted her.

He mounted the mare while she lay there and she immediately jumped up, Jonathan holding tight to the reins. He laughed at himself, "You thought I couldn't do that, didn't you girl." he said.

For his whole life, he had always been frightened of horses. He had been until he had met Lillian, who could handle horses better than anyone he had ever seen. She had taught him not to fear them, but Patrick and then Peter had taught him to love them. Now he felt more comfortable riding than walking, especially since, at times, his mended, broken leg still bothered him.

He rode quietly back down the hill he had climbed and turned upriver to where he could access the riverbank without the soldiers in the camp seeing him. He would wait there until dark and then cross the river and ride the short distance to the cliff walls. They had once been several days journey away. However, they were now just across the river itself. The Shadow Realm was shrinking, he thought.

There was a break in the foliage by the river and Jonathan rode to the tree line and dismounted. There was still at least an hour before sunset, and he would wait for the cover of darkness before crossing the river. He left the mare under the trees and climbed down the bank to the water's edge where he could see across the river. The far side was void of trees at this point but covered with a high tumble of large rocks that had recently fallen from the high cliffs above, crashing down on the trees that had been there and tearing them from the ground, utterly devastating the forest. Even as he watched, a large boulder crashed down the cliff walls and landed in the river with a tremendous splash.

Jonathan spied out a route he could take to cross the river and work his way past the cliff walls in the dark. He climbed back up the bank to where the horse waited. Jonathan had planned to leave the horse by the river and after finding Lillian, to return and escape on horseback, but he changed his mind.

"Well girl, this is where we part ways," he said as he took a pencil and paper and wrote a note to Peter, warning of the army and saying that as soon as he rescued Lillian, he would return. He also explained that the entire Shadow Realm seemed to be pulling in on itself and if it continued, the distance between the armies would be minimal.

Jonathan placed the note in a protective covering and tied it to the saddle. He then removed the sword and a small satchel that held a bit of food, water, and the journal. Jonathan kept the horse close and petted the side of her face.

"You go home, girl. Run as fast as you can and go home. I will see you again. I promise," Jonathan said and stepped back.

The horse nodded her head and turned, and with one last look over her shoulder, she bolted across the plains and soon disappeared behind the hills. With sadness, Jonathan watched her run. She had been his companion since he had arrived at Soteria, he thought, and he had never even given her a proper name.

He turned and climbed back down the riverbank to the water's edge. Downstream he saw movement on the far bank. He would wait for darkness and then swim across the river. With any luck, he could find Lillian and get back out before daylight. He had no idea what he would do. He did not even know if she was guarded or not. All he knew was that she was held captive in the valley behind the cliffs.

The Light brightened at his chest with his growing faith, and he knew that he would know what to do when the time came.

MACKENZIE'S JOURNAL
DAY NINE

This is too much for me. Is this real truth or just the ramblings of myself? Truth comes in all forms my son. I am the Way, the Truth and the Life. I spoke to my disciples, and they wrote it down. So why can't I do the same now with you? Believe in what you have been teaching.

All beauty is God-given, God ordained. I create all beauty. In fact, all things, good or bad as a man thinks are created by me. It is what you do with it that makes it good or bad.

I breathe on man's hands, and they paint, blow in their mouth, and they sing, pulse through their muscles, and they run, they build, they create, they write. You are created in my image. Therefore, you are meant to create. Even people who do not know me, their souls have not awakened to my presence, even these people create, and I am pleased with man's creativity.

But when a soul awakens to my presence, when a person becomes a new creation in Christ, then my true self comes forth. My people were meant to be the most creative of all, and I rejoice over the pure dance, the song, the written word, laughter, helping hands, compassion, and true love. When you truly understand the Kingdom of God within you, the God-given creativity that is in all humanity, the very creative passion that is in me that lives within you. When you become a new creation and awaken to my presence, then you will understand that everything you do, whether great works of art or just the minuscule works of everyday life is a celebration of my creativity in you.

Truly you and I become one, the way it was meant to be when I first walked in the garden with you. Know that everything you do, whether small or great, I can take glory in if you open your heart to my spirit, open your soul to my grace, my love, and my creativity.

Enjoy the life I give you. Enjoy the time I give you.

Know this that I rejoice over you, my most beautiful of creative beings. I am your Father. I look at you as you do your children. When they were small, they would draw you a picture, make you a toy, play in your house, your yard, and create unimaginable creations. Remember how they looked? The cat did not look like a cat, but you loved the picture anyway and placed it on the refrigerator for all to see. Because of their innocence, they created what they wanted to create.

It is the same with you. All I ask is that you who are created in my image learn to create in your world. Just enjoy my house. Do your best. I will take care of the rest.

There is a point in a man's life when he strives to become something that he was never meant to be. Beware of this time and focus on me, your Father. Become what I designed you to be and your frustration will disappear. Learn to follow me. Your day of gloom seems to overwhelm you, but never let it. Remember time is just a season. The darkness today will turn into sunshine just as quickly. Remember that I am in your despair just as I am in your sunshine. Take the trials of life as things that happen. They are fleeting. They are vapor. Rains today, sunshine comes quickly. Remember that I am in the rain and the sunshine. It is the same with trying days and restful ones. I live with you in both.

Consider it all joy. Know that I am your God, your creator. I lead you in the right paths, even when they travel through adversity. I can still lead you on the path. You have to walk the lighted path that I have provided.

See the new life sprouting forth in the trees, the beautiful spring flowers, the birds hatching forth under their mother's protective wings. The life is beautiful, happy, and content even under the dark, gloomy sky.

My creation responds to the storms the same way it responds to the warm afternoon sunshine. My creation anticipates the change and continues life through both.

CHAPTER EIGHTEEN

As the sun slipped behind the mountains and the river became lost in the shadows of the cliffs, Jonathan silently moved into the water. The water was icy, the current strong and deep. He gripped the floating log he had spotted on the bank and pushed out into the current, allowing the current to pull him downstream as he swam. Halfway across, he realized that he was traveling to far toward the camp and let go of the log, took a deep breath and ducked under the surface so he could swim as hard as he could against the current without making any noise.

The water was dark, murky and full of leaves, twigs and other debris. He could not see under the water, but he could tell when he was nearing the far shore as the current lessened. Jonathan reached forward in the darkness until he found the bank and then slowly rose above the water in total darkness. He climbed up the bank and found himself in the middle of the rockslide. Although the rocks would make travel more difficult, they provided abundant cover, and the chances of anyone being in the area were very minimal.

Jonathan could see very little in the darkness, only shadows of the rocks and trees, the glistening water and the high looming cliffs above him. Far off down the river, hundreds of campfires glowed. He carefully maneuvered through the boulder field for a few hundred yards before suddenly emerging out into a meadow with several nomad tents along one side near the river and a massive campfire between. Several nomads sat by the fire eating, talking and laughing. Jonathan watched for a few minutes, thinking of the good times that he had enjoyed while with Captain Connelly's clan. He wondered if they were somewhere among the nomad tents.

One of the men stood up and walked into the fire's light, holding his hands out to warm them, and Jonathan was shocked to see that he appeared not to have any chains around him. The last time he had been with the nomads when he had activated the Light and witnessed the vision of the cross and the slain lamb, he had seen the nomads in their true form, men and women covered in chains and dying. Several others walked into the fire's light, and they only had a few links around them. They appeared not to know they were chained because of the deception, but something was definitely changing. Why were they losing their chains like the fugitives?

Jonathan clasped the Light around his neck, feeling its warmth and strength. Before as with Heather, Patrick and Peter, Jonathan had to give them the Light for it to be activated. When Krino was defeated, who was the Archon of the fugitives, all fugitives suddenly found themselves free of the chains of death and showed up at the river crossing each day. But the nomads were not affected, or maybe he had been wrong. After all, the inhabitants of Hedone had disappeared and the city destroyed. The entire Shadow Realm was somehow falling apart around him. And now something was happening with the nomads even though they were still living under some power of deception.

Too many things were happening that Jonathan did not understand, and he did not have time to worry about them now, he thought. He had to find Lillian. Jonathan ambled past the tents along the cliff wall until he came to a wooden palisade which was the Nomad Council House. Two nomad guards stood by the only gateway and Jonathan stopped. How could he get past the guards?

"JUST WALK RIGHT THROUGH THE DOOR."

Jonathan drew his sword and then realized that the Light had not told him to do that, so he placed it quietly back in the sheath and boldly took a step out in the fading light from one of the warming fires nearly. He fully expected the guards to challenge him, but they appeared not to see him. He walked a little more confidently up to the two men who stared directly forward.

Suddenly a large boulder fell from the cliffs above, tearing in the palisade wall and the guards jumped back and looked away, and Jonathan slipped past them and through the busted gate. Jonathan realized when he entered the walled area that the guards stood guard over a gateway that led to an abandoned courtyard and broken-down council houses. More mystery, he thought. And he suddenly felt an overpowering urge that it was time to draw the sword, which he immediately did.

Across the ruined courtyard, there appeared to be an opening in the cliff walls. Just inside the cavern entrance, two torches cast dancing orange lights that helped illuminate the blackness of the cave. Jonathan carefully made his way quietly through a maze of broken furniture and tables. Scattered across the ground were clothing, jewels, gold and half rotten food. He was reminded of how the courtyard at Hedone had looked when he first entered there. It was as if something terrible had scared all the inhabitants away right in the middle of some festival.

Jonathan peered into the cavern and could only see a few feet to where it appeared the tunnel turned. He hesitated at the door. The tunnel could lead to Lillian, or it could lead to his destruction, he thought. But he had to trust in what he had seen, of what the voice had spoken to him.

Suddenly the rocks above him trembled; dirt began to fall around him, and then rocks. He jumped back from the opening and then lunged forward as a section of the rock wall collapsed around him. He fell into the cave, dropping the sword and covering his head as the cave opening disappeared in a tumble of rock and dirt.

Jonathan lay there for a moment, waiting as the ground shook and landside subsided. He lay in total blackness among a jumble of rock and debris. He pushed himself away from the pile of dirt and felt around the ground for the sword, which he eventually found a few feet away.

Suddenly the heaviness of the darkness around him caused him to breath faster, his heart beating wildly, as panic and fear began to take control of his mind. He had not felt such fear since way before in the dark cave before he had ever found the Light. What was happening to him? Jonathan reached for the Light around his neck and realized with a sudden fear that the Light was not there.

All around him, he saw black shadows even darker than the total darkness dancing around, floating. He held the sword in front of him and backed into the wall, trembling at what he saw. What terror awaited him in the tunnels? He thought. He had to take control of himself. The Light had to be somewhere, but where? So much was changing around him. The Shadow Realm was disappearing, and he did not know if that was a good thing or bad? What would happen when everything finally disappeared? Where would he be? Where would anyone that he knew be?

Jonathan closed his eyes and focused on the Light itself and not on the black shadows that swirled around him. He had to get control over himself. Every time before, the Light glowed outward and revealed what lay behind the darkness. Now it had suddenly disappeared. The rules were changing, he thought. The Shadow Realm was shrinking around him, and the rules were changing.

He thought of the strange place he had landed when he first rode into the monuments and followed the shaft of light through the door. He appeared in another realm where the rules were different, where the Light appeared to be everywhere all at once. Was that happening here? But there was no Light, or was there?

"THE TRUE KINGDON IS BEYOND ALL YOU SEE. ALL WILL BE REVEALED SOON."

Jonathan was used to the voice now and had learned to trust it. He stood up and opened his eyes. The Light still hung around his neck as it has always done, glowing brightly, but at the same time, the tunnel itself seemed to fill with its presence in a way that had never happened before in the Shadow Realm. He cautiously walked further into the darkness, feeling along the wall until it turned and the orange light from the torches that lighted each side of the wall almost blinded him. The new tunnel led straight into the mountain for nearly a hundred feet before turning again.

He listened carefully but heard nothing but the low crackling of the torches. Behind him was total darkness and the cave was blocked, so at least he did not have to worry about what lay behind him. He continued down the tunnel until the turn and walked through a broken door into a large chamber room. In the center of the room stood a fountain, full of water, with cascading falls coming down from far above. Jonathan looked up into the darkness but could not see where the water came from. It just fell from nothingness above.

There were four doors in the room, each one located at the four cardinal directions, north, south, east and west. The room was lighted by four large torches, one by each of the doors. He had come into the room through the south door, which had lain broken. The two side doors appeared to be solid, but the one across from him, the north door, lay open. A darkened tunneled led past the north door.

Jonathan checked each of the side doors and confirmed that both were solid and locked with a chain, leaving only one way in which he could travel. He knew that the north door led to Lillian.

He could feel her presence close by and the thought of being united with her once again elated him. Would she accept him? Or would she hate him for what had happened to her?

Jonathan cautiously walked through the tunnel, keeping to the inside wall as the tunnel curved almost back on itself, it seemed until suddenly he saw daylight in front of him. He would have to be careful, he thought. Surely there were guards stationed at the entrance.

He crept to the door until he stood just inside the opening. Outside revealed a beautiful valley filled with trees and open, flower-covered meadows. The sunshine was warm, and the valley appeared to be in the full throes of spring, in stark contrast to where he had just come from. What place was this? What garden was this? He thought.

To one side, Jonathan saw a stone house surrounded by flower gardens and graveled walkways. Birds sang from the trees and fluttered around in front of him. Deer ranged peacefully out in the meadow. He waited and watched but saw no one and then he thought he heard the faint sound of harp music, playing off in the distance.

"She's locked in the room upstairs," a female voice startled Jonathan, and he swirled suddenly, sword in hand.

A young servant girl stood under the trees. She had not been there just seconds before, or had she?

"Who's in the room?" Jonathan asked.

"You know who she is," the girl answered and then asked, "You are the Apostolos Or, aren't you?"

Jonathan vaguely recognized the young girl but could not place from where. Some distant memory lay just under the surface, just beyond his grasp, like most of his memories now did.

"Yes. I suppose I am," Jonathan asked.

The girl nodded her head and smiled, "I knew that you would show up after the girl arrived. She has remembered you. At first, she hated you for leaving her, but now I think she understands more than even you do."

Jonathan looked at the girl, confused. What was she talking about? He looked around him again, thinking that maybe this was a trap.

"Don't worry. The guards are all inside. There are six of them, two at each door. You go through the back door to the house. There are two just inside the first door, two at the bottom of the stairs and two at the upstairs room where the girl is."

Could he believe her? Jonathan thought for a moment. He had to know more before he could entirely trust this girl.

"What is this place?" he asked. "And who are you?"

"This is the home of Archon Planos and Zanah. You met them once before, you know."

"What do you mean?" Jonathan asked, perplexed.

"By the fire when the girl was taken away. When you first brought the Light among us. Remember, she rode up to you by the wagons."

Jonathan thought of the warrior woman who had tried to seduce him the very night he had activated the Light. Malak had broken her spell, and he had taken Heather and ran into the Monuments of Life where he had first met Patrick and Peter. How did this girl know about that?

"How do you know about that?" Jonathan asked, suddenly distrustful of the girl. What magic was this?

The girl took a step closer, and he saw fear in her eyes for the first time, "That does not matter. Just remember that you must be united with the girl again for the three of us to be saved. You are the Apostolos Or. You have brought the Light among us. Now you must unite us all under the Light's power."

And the girl suddenly disappeared.

MACKENZIE'S JOURNAL
DAY TEN

My thoughts are jumbled. I think that I hear from you God, but the words don't make sense at times......

It's okay son. The more that you learn what my voice truly sounds like, the more you know that the words you hear and write down are truly mine. Just write what you hear. The rest is my responsibility. Just like the journey called life. I meant for my creation, mankind, created after my image to live life in the same manner. Faith of a small child. Follow me along the path of life. Create a mosaic of beauty and worship. Even though days of trouble, learn to fly the bird dance even through the darkening skies. Watch flocks of birds, dancing majestically across the sky. My dance that I breathe into their little bodies. They fly in majestic dance through the clouds as well as through the sunshine. They don't care which; they only care that they can fly. My longing for you is that you will enjoy the dance that I have breathed in you. Don't look at the gloom or sunshine except to see that both show my glory. Only rejoice that I have breathed the dance of life in your soul.

When you awaken to my spirit that lives within you, when you truly feel my kingdom in your mortal bodies, then you can fully appreciate the dance that I have placed within you. And even on days when the pressures of this life are upon you, you can focus on the dance. And you and I can fly together through the gloom and the sunshine, partners in life, my true love, my most precious creation.

My heart yearns to fly in unison with all my children, the same way that I fly in unison with the multitude of birds that you see in your world every day. Rejoice in the dance, rejoice in my love for you, rejoice in the love you feel by kindred spirits that are all around you, rejoice in the family I have placed you in.

Be content with where I place you in ministry. Everyone has their place in the kingdom. All are equally important in my eyes, even though in your eyes they may not seem to be so. Learn to function in the calling and season that I have ordained for you. Your true identity should be in me, not in what you do for me. Then when I direct you to other areas or forms of ministry for my kingdom, you still will be confident and secure in who you are. You are my child, my creation. All that you do for me, I am proud of. Place your focus on me through Jesus, not what you do for me. Funnel all that you are through Jesus. Make Him the center of all that you are. Then your identity will become strong, and you will truly become one with me. Just as Jesus prayed. He prayed for you to be one with him the same as he is one with me. Set your focus on Jesus and then your true destiny will spring forth like never before.

I take delight in all my children do for me. The pure heart will trust me completely and be content in the position that I have placed him in my kingdom. Remember that there is a season for all things. That is true in the work of the kingdom. As you learn to be content in the little things, the minor details, I will open the big things over your life. Learn to listen to my words, words directly from me to your soul through the Holy Spirit.

The noise of life in your existence can overcome at times the words of life that I speak into your spirit. You must learn to shield your ears from the noise of life around you so that you can hear the words of life that are spoken over you.

CHAPTER NINETEEN

Jonathan stared at the place where the girl had stood under the trees and then just as quickly vanished from sight, or had she just hidden quickly behind the thickets. He clasped the Light and felt reassured by the Light's warmth. Once again, he was utterly perplexed by the changes that had occurred around him.

The crumbling Shadow Realm, the abandoned village, the tunnels and now this beautiful garden, so peaceful and pure, all seemed so real, yet at the same time, an illusion. And then the girl appeared, telling him things that she should not have known. Who was she? He thought. He remembered her from somewhere, sometime in the past, but could not pin the fleeting memory down.

But at the same time, Jonathan felt Lillian somewhere close. Her presence seemed to fill the entire valley. The girl said that he would have to unite with her to save them all.

The stone house was only a short distance through the trees and Jonathan walked slowly and quietly across the graveled path and into the shadows of the thickets created as the sun began to lose itself behind the fog above the mountains. The girl had said that there was a total of six guards, two at each door. He would have to fight his way through, he thought. But maybe there was another way.

Jonathan walked around to the back of the structure facing the setting sun and sighted a balcony high up above the tallest trees. It was the only balcony and must be the upstairs room the girl had told him about. He stood in the shadows and studied the rock wall. He could climb that wall, he thought. He had rock climbed many times. He could climb the wall and possibly find a way to escape back out through the window.

Jonathan could feel her presence. He knew that Lillian had to be in the room, but he dared not call out to her and expose himself to the guards. The hole in his being ached with the knowledge that Lillian had been the missing part of his existence and with renewed exhilaration, he knew that they would soon be together again.

Up in her room, Lillian suddenly doubled over as a shooting pain slashed through her side and then was replaced by a warm sensation of peace. Jonathan was near, she thought. The vacant place in her being that she could not understand, she now knew without a doubt was her desire to be reunited with him. All her past doubts, all of the deception, all that she had experienced in the valley suddenly was exposed for what they were. Lies. She stood up from the bed and faced the window. He was out there, just beyond the window, and he was climbing to her.

Lillian first thought she would rush to the window and call out to him, but then remembered the guards who she could hear just outside her door. She walked quietly over to the closed window and opened it. The darkness was now complete with the disappearance of the sun, and she could only hear someone climbing up the rock wall below her. She leaned over the wall and saw a figure about halfway up the wall below her.

Jonathan climbed slowly up the wall, the stone structure construction creating plentiful hand and feet holds. He looked up once and saw someone just out of sight who was opening the window. With renewed strength, he quickened his pace. After a few more feet, he grabbed the lower railing and pulled himself over and on to the balcony.

Lillian stood by the open window, her small hand covering her mouth in surprise. Jonathan stood there transfixed by her beauty. The last time he had seen her, she had been dragged away by the nomads as the camp was being raided. With sadness, he also remembered how she had slapped him, cursing him and blaming him for the destruction. He knew that the deception blinded her and that she believed that all the nomads were free of their chains. He had so desperately wanted to go back and save her, then give her the Light and let it free her as it had freed him. But Malak had said that it was not time.

And now she stood before him as beautiful as the first time he had seen her when the clan had saved him from the desert and brought him into their camp. He did not know what to say, what to do next. Awkwardly, he stood there in the darkness.

"I climbed the wall," was all he could say.

Lillian laughed and rushed to him, embracing him tightly, "You came. I always knew that you would come."

Jonathan returned her embrace, burying his face in her hair, breathing in her intoxicating presence. They embraced for what seemed an eternity before the Light suddenly glowed brilliantly, illuminating the entire balcony and the girl stepped away.

The Light pulsed strongly as Jonathan had seen it do several times before it would transform someone and remove their chains, but Lillian had no chains. The last time he had been with her, the Light had shown her true form, a girl covered in chains the way he had been, but now she glowed radiantly in the Light's illumination.

"Oh, it is stunning, Jonathan. I was so wrong to doubt you before. Will you give it to me now? I truly do wish to be free of these chains." the girl begged.

And suddenly Jonathan realized that something was not quite right. The girl standing before him had no chains. The Light always revealed the truth. Why had she begged to be free of her chains when this girl had no chains around her? Jonathan backed away, staring at the girl before him.

"What's wrong, love. Please let me hold the Light," the girl asked, holding out her hand, staring intently through him with her seductively bright green eyes. "You can free me from my chains, and we can live in this paradise forever together. This garden is such a beautiful place, is it not? With my chains removed, you and I can be lovers forever."

Jonathan backed away again to the very edge of the balcony. He glanced around and behind him but saw nothing but the shadows of the trees in the moon's light and then suddenly a form appeared below him on the wall and then two more. He reached for his sword just as a blackness fell over him with incredible weight and the girl before him transformed into the green-eyed woman he had first encountered on the night when he had first activated the Light.

MACKENZIE'S JOURNAL
DAY ELEVEN

Oh God, who are you in this world?

I am all things. I created all things. I am all around you. I look at you from the clouds you see, the flowers I created, the animals that run in my forests. All was created by me and for me. But I stand above them all. My creation always points to me, but at times people only stop at my creation. They can't see past it to me even though my creation screams my existence in all that it does.

However, when your soul truly awakens to my presence, then you can see me in all that I have created. When my children are not awakened to my presence, they become slaves to my creation around them. They are fearful. They lose all hope. They are taken by the evil of this world. They only see the creation in its fallen state. The laws of nature speak life and death, sickness and health, good and evil. And people become trapped within these laws.

But that is not how it was originally meant to be. You are no longer under the law. You are covered by my grace, my mercy, and my love. See the creation the way that I meant it to be, and you will no longer be enslaved by its natural laws. Learn to look into the eyes of my greatest creation, man, and see past the laws of nature that are currently present in your world and you will see me looking back into your eyes.

When you see all mankind the way I intended them to be, then you will see the destiny that lies within them. But before you can see me in all the people around you, you must first see inside of your soul. So, it comes back to identity. Mankind's true identity is not found in my creation, it is found in me.

Religion has made me something that I never wanted to be. Yes, I am above all things. I am the God of all my creation. I sit on a throne above all that you could ever know. But my heart is to be as one with my creation. I chose to leave all that I am, to dwell in the temple that I created in you for my presence.

Religion places walls up. I tear walls down

Religion places me outside of man's reach. I reach out and bring man into myself.

Religion places man back under the law of creation that is still in a fallen state. I pull man out of the fallen state and make each one a new creation.

Religion says that you must constantly strive under the law to reach me. I leave my throne and choose to walk hand in hand with you, in your world.

I did not have to create you. I chose to create you. Then you and I can have true fellowship with each other.

My words of life are lamps to guide your steps through your world. Religion has made my words shackles that keep you bound. But my words offer freedom to live above the world.

CHAPTER TWENTY

Lillian stood by the open window, her small hand covering her mouth in surprise as the form jumped over the railing and stood before her. It was the servant girl, Gloria. Lillian had fully expected Jonathan. She was sure of it. She felt his presence all around her, even as Gloria stood there in front of her.

"Gloria, what are you...." she paused in disbelief. Even though she saw Gloria before her, she felt Jonathan so close to her that she thought she could reach out and touch him.

"It's okay mistress. He is here, very close, but Zanah has set a trap for him. He came to save us, but now it is you that must save us. Do you wish us to be free, mistress?" the girl asked.

Lillian backed away as the girl walked past her and into the room, "Of course, Gloria, with all that I am, I wish to be free."

"Good," Gloria stated with a strong finality, "Then we must go to him now before it is too late."

Gloria looked around the room until she saw what she needed. She took a chair and hit it against the bed, breaking off the legs. She kept one for herself and gave the other to Lillian as Lillian stood watching her in total amazement.

"For most of my life, I was a slave in the Shadow Realm, bound by law to, in time destroy myself, but then the Apostolos Or came with the Light and then you came as well and now I have a voice in my own life. I can now do my part to help save us," Gloria stated as she stood there defiantly, holding the chair leg like a sword.

Lillian smiled at her tenacity and balanced her chair leg as well. Her father had taught her how to handle a sword, but she had never done so in battle. But what were they to do now?

"Gloria, where is he? I know he is close. I can feel his presence like he is standing right beside me." Lillian asked.

"He was climbing to your room mistress," Gloria answered.

"But I am in my room, Gloria" Lillian exclaimed and then looked around her. She was not in her room. She was standing next to the table in the veranda, where she had last eaten with Zanah.

Gloria gasped in confusion, "But you were in your room. I saw you leave. I told Jonathan that you were there and that there were guards at each of the doors to the house!"

"It's okay, Gloria. It appears that Zanah has bewitched us all with her deception."

The two looked toward the house and the open doorway. There were no guards there now. They both began to run to the house and quickly found themselves in the long hallway that led to the stairs. It was dark, so they had to be careful as they found the bottom of the steps and slowly navigated their way up to the bedroom door.

They both hesitated at the closed door. A strange white light glowed from around the door itself. It was the same type of light that Lillian remembered seeing around Jonathon on that night long ago when she had also seen the image of a man standing behind him. Gloria too had seen the Light once, long ago for just a moment, before it had been snatched from her. They could hear a struggle inside and with a firm push; they opened the door and fell into the Light itself.

They heard a woman scream, "Nooo!"

And there was a great crash and a flashing sword, and then they lay in the trees under the balcony itself among the garden. Jonathan stood over them, panting heavily, holding the sword with both hands, the blade tip embedded in the soft dirt.

All three stared in disbelief at each other, thinking the same thing. What had just happened?

Jonathan stared in disbelief at the two forms before him. Lillian lay on her back. The servant girl lay beside her on her side. Both held what appeared to be chair legs.

"You saved me," was all he could say.

Lillian set up, staring up at him and held her arms out, dropping the chair leg. Jonathon grabbed her up in his arms and hugged her deeply. She was dirty, her clothes were tattered, her hair was messy and tangled, and the chains covered her body, but Jonathan had never seen a more beautiful woman in his entire life. For the first time, since he had last seen her, he felt entirely whole.

He kissed her, and she returned the kiss, and they hugged each other again until the Light suddenly glowed strongly around them as Gloria stood up quietly. Lillian stood back suddenly and looked down at her as the Light covered her body and one by one, the chains fell away from her. She stared up at Jonathan, her eyes sparkling, her face radiantly beautiful and suddenly there were flowers in her hair. And she hugged him again.

"Excuse the interruption, you two, but we have a problem," Gloria stated and pointed to the house where dozens of soldiers suddenly appeared from the doorway.

Jonathan knew that they were not quite safe yet and had to somehow get out of the valley and back to the others. The only way he knew was back to the tunnels. Hopefully one of the other closed doors led back to the river.

"Okay, quick now! We need to get back to the tunnel. There has to be a way out through one of the doors!"

The three began running through the path toward the cliff walls as Zanah shouted for the soldiers to kill them all. An armored warrior suddenly jumped at them from behind a tree and Gloria struck him with the chair leg, knocking him back and allowing Jonathan to thrust his broadsword, knocking the man down. Another stood before them at the tunnel entrance, thrusting a spear. Jonathan parried the blow, sidestepped quickly and slashed down and across the man, killing him instantly.

They entered the tunnel just as a dozen arrows thudded around them against the rock wall and fell harmlessly to the ground.

"This way!" Jonathan ordered, and they ran deeper into the tunnels until they found themselves once more in the chamber room with the cascading waterfalls.

The three circled the fountains, frantically looking for a way out, but there was only one closed door. Jonathan was confused. When he had first entered the chamber, there had been four doors, two open and two closed. Now there were just two. One they had just come out of and one a closed wooden door locked with a chain.

"Where do we go, Jonathan?" Lillian asked

"I truly don't know," Jonathan answered.

Lillian stepped in front of Jonathan and took hold of his hand, "There is another way out of the valley, Jonathan. I saw a mountain range, a city on a hill with people and animals. It appeared through a gap in the fog beyond the cliffs. When I first saw it, I heard a voice. It said virtue, peace, and joy. And then another time I heard it say that the true kingdom is out there. I did not know where the voice came from, but now I know." she said as she clasped the Light around her neck.

Jonathan remembered the strange place he had found himself when he had first entered the monuments as he journeyed in search of Lillian. The place where he had been given the journal that he had been reading ever since. There was definitely a new kingdom out there, but how could they get to it now.

"You know the way?" Jonathan asked.

"Yes, I think so, but we have to go back out into the valley," Lillian answered.

"I think it is too late," Gloria stated the obvious as the room suddenly filled up with soldiers.

The men stopped suddenly across from the fountain, staring at the water as if it was poison. Jonathan looked around him and suddenly noticed a white glow of light shining from the space beneath the closed door. He took the sword and slashed down against the chains, and the door suddenly broke away and disappeared, revealing a forest. They all three immediately knew that the door was indeed a way into the other kingdom, whatever that kingdom was.

"Quick! inside!" Jonathan ordered, and Lillian immediately stepped inside, but Gloria held back.

"Come on girl, that is the only way out!"

"I can't. It is not my time yet. You must go. You are the Apostolos Or. I will be fine here until the appointed time now that you and she are together."

"What do you mean? We have to go!" Jonathan grabbed for the girl, but she stepped back.

"No Jonathan. Don't you know who I am?" Gloria stared at him defiantly.

She reminded him of some distant memory, something horrible from long ago. And then suddenly he knew who she was. She was the girl in the cave. She was the girl who had a portion of the Light who had begged him to save her as he hid. She was the girl that the Sahat had stripped the Light from and then had killed her, or so he had always thought. How could that be?

"But how can that be?" Jonathan stammered, so ashamed to be in her presence.

"How can you ever forgive me? I let you die that night."

Gloria smiled, "No, you saved me that night. That was the night that you found the Light. The night that you first became alive."

"But all of that doesn't matter now. You have to go with us." Jonathan pleaded.

"I can't at this time. That way leads to a new kingdom. I must stay here for a little while longer, but that is fine with me because I know that you and she are together now. When the time comes, we will all be together again, like we were meant to be."

"I still do not understand why you can't come with us?"

"Because Jonathan, I belong here in the Shadow Realm, and the reason why I belong in the Shadow Realm, is because I am the Shadow Realm," she stated and kicked him violently into the door as it crumbled behind him.

MACKENZIE'S JOURNAL
DAY TWELVE

God speak to me. Help me always to hear your voice in my spirit…..

I wish to be practical in your everyday experience. I am seen by men at times only as a God of the supernatural, and I am. However, I wish to bring the supernatural of my existence directly into the physical flesh and blood of your existence. The Kingdom of God invades the physical world with the supernatural. For the Kingdom of God to truly become active in your life, you need to understand that I wish to be active in all aspects of your life. We walk together in the spiritual realms, and that is good. That is the true reality of your world. However, you must also allow me to walk with you in the physical world as well.

How can that be, you ask? The true reality of the kingdom is spiritual because I am Spirit and so are you, but you live in a physical body. I wish to be practical in all areas of your life. Allow me to direct your path in all areas of life.

Your soul walks with me in the garden in the cool of the day, and I love the fellowship and the relationship that we have. Now let me help you in the physical world. Listen to my words. Seek my advice. I wish for you to allow me to assist you in the everyday activities of your life.

CHAPTER TWENTY ONE

Jonathan fell through the opening and out into a thickly forested glade, hard on his face, his sword dropping further down the hill below him. He covered his face as rocks pelted his head and back as the tunnel collapsed behind him, He lay there stunned at what the girl had revealed to him before she kicked him through the door. She made absolutely no sense, he thought. How could she be the Shadow Realm, when the Shadow Realm was all around him? She had to be crazy, he thought. But then again, he knew for a fact that she was indeed the same girl who he had first encountered in the cave of his fears when he had first encountered the Light. He had seen her killed by the Sahat on that terrible night, but she had told him that he had saved her.

Jonathan instinctively grabbed for the Light around his neck, and with panic, realized that it no longer felt warm to the touch. He looked down and realized that it was only a rock and had no light at all. He looked around him, trying to understand where he had fallen into and knew after a moment, that once again, he had somehow crossed over into another dimension where the Light was all around him all at the same time. It lived and breathed in everything around him, and he felt its warm and comforting presence in the very air itself.

"Lillian," he called, but there was no answer.

"Welcome back, friend," a voice spoke from behind him, and Jonathan turned quickly and stood up, backing away from the voice that he had heard.

The man he had seen by the ocean gate stood before him, smiling widely and holding out his hand in greeting. Jonathan stood for a moment, perplexed as he fought to remember the man's name.

"Crestos? Keeper of the Wall?" Jonathan asked.

"Yes, you remembered." Crestos remarked, "And you are the Apostolos Or, or in my language, Pneuma, but I believe you called yourself Jonathan before."

"Yes sir," Jonathan answered, completely taken back by the man standing before him, "Sir, a girl came through just ahead of me. I need to find her. We have to get back to help our friends and warn them."

"Yes, the girl, Lillian, she called herself. Such a beautiful lady. In my language, she is called Psuche, but Lillian will do for now. You have done well to share the Light with her."

"Where is she? She fell through the door just moments before I did. She has to be close!" Jonathan exclaimed. Where could she have gone?

"Jonathan, she came through over a week ago, but don't worry. My counterpart is with her. His name is Eleos, and he will lead her through the journey that only she can travel,"

That could not be, Jonathan thought. They had just been in the tunnel. Jonathan looked around him. For as far as he could see, massive trees grew over a bed of flowers and lush grass, trees more magnificent than any he had ever seen. The place reminded him of the valley that he had just left, but there was one thing that this place had that the other valley did not. In the valley, he had felt a sort of peace, but it seemed an illusion and upon seeing Lillian, a joy that was incomprehensible, however, now he felt a total purity that the valley was missing and peace that was beyond comprehension. Lillian had said of the kingdom she had seen that it was made up of virtue, peace, and joy. Was this the kingdom she had seen through the gap?

Crestos saw the confusion in Jonathan's eyes and walked over and placed his hands on Jonathan's shoulders to comfort him. Jonathan immediately trusted the man and desperately needed to know that everything was okay.

"Jonathan, I know that so much has happened that you do not understand, but in time you will. Now you see through a glass darkly, but in time you will see all with great clarity. You have brought the Light to the Shadow Realm, and you have freed her. You have given her the strength to overcome and every day the Shadow Realm shrinks because you have shined the Light in the darkness. You worry about your friends who are still in the Shadow Realm. They still have the battle to fight, but in time, even that battle will come to an end and you The Apostolos Or, and Lillian will be there together."

Jonathan did not fully understand what Crestos was telling him, but he did realize that even though he could not see Lillian with him now, he knew that she was with him anyway. Because the significant gap in his very being that had been vacant since she had been pulled away from him by the river was now full and they were somehow united, and he felt her presence and knew that she felt his.

"The Light told both me and Lillian that there was a kingdom out there. Is this the kingdom the Light spoke of?" Jonathan.

Crestos stared intently into Jonathan's eyes, "Partially Jonathan. Like you saw by the ocean, this land is only a portion of the total kingdom that awaits you. But don't worry; you have done your job well. Now it is Lillian's time to overcome in this land. There are still dangers out there because even in this kingdom, the curse can have power if you let it, but she is totally secure in King Elohim's arms. And in the final Garden, there is no curse."

"But can't I help her! I have just found her. I do not want to lose her again," Jonathan pleaded.

"Jonathan, you will not lose her. You are already with her. It is her time now, and then both of you will see what the Shadow Realm had become together, arm in arm, the way you were created to be before the curse came upon mankind."

And Crestos touched Jonathan on the forehead, and suddenly Jonathan found himself high on a mountain precipice overlooking the entire world, it seemed. Far below he saw the forest, the wild canyons, the distant ocean and then he saw Lillian and knew that she would have to face the trail herself, but he was with her even though he could only see her from the mountaintop. He felt the incredible presence of the Light, but in this kingdom, the Light filled everything, and there was a presence so strong that he looked around him to see if Elohim himself stood beside him.

He knew the Light was the Light of the World, the slain Lamb of God that he had seen in the Shadow Realm in person when the Light had removed his chains. In this dimension, whatever this place was, the Light was more than before but was still not entirely present in a physical form that he could see and touch. But that was okay. He knew that now he saw through a glass darkly, but one day he would see with total clarity. He was content, filled with virtue, peace, and joy, even though he still knew that in the Shadow Realm, the forces were massing for an attack on Soteria itself.

But the realm that Jonathan and Lillian found themselves in was still only a shadow of the truth itself. Although holding a glimpse of the eternal, it was still scarred somewhat by the curse of mankind that would be redeemed when the truth was revealed. However now, hidden among the forest and canyons, powers lay dormant that could overpower those who traveled through, if they allowed them to. The soul of man could be a temperamental thing, often bowing to the emotions, the passions, the fears of life, just as the Shadow Realm could.

Zanah knew this, and although angered beyond control when the two had escaped the delusion of her valley, she knew exactly where they had traveled. Her plan to take the Light from Jonathan had failed, but she knew that she still had a chance to separate them before it was too late.

Archon Planos stood over the valley watching his troops assemble as Zanah rode up to him, her eyes wild with anger, "They escaped through the tunnels!" was all she could say.

Somehow her magic spell had been broken. The girl had somehow been able to see through the delusion to the kingdom beyond the fog. And just when she had the Apostolos Or where she could take the Light from him, the servant girl had crashed through the door. How could that be? The servant girl, the very one who had no power at all, had broken through the door and suddenly they were all gone.

"It does not matter, Zanah," Archon Planos stated, "We will destroy the army of the Apostolos Or, and it will all be over. We will destroy the Shadow Realm along with its army. It has already begun."

Archon Planos waved his arm in front of him, and for the first time, Zanah saw what the Shadow Realm had become. The mountains were falling in among themselves; the distances across the great plains were shrinking. The Forest of Basar was only a short distance from where they now stood. Soon Soteria itself would be within their reach.

"But the Light still has power. We must destroy it." Zanah pleaded.

"Then go and do your worst. I will take care of the army," Archon Planos ordered.

Zanah spurred her horse onward, back to the valley. She knew a way through the broken portals to the half-world where Jonathan and Lillian escaped to. She still had a chance, she thought. She still had power over the souls of mankind. And even though the Apostolos Or had revealed the Light to Lillian, the soul was weak at times, and Zanah would attack her directly. Let Planos destroy the Shadow Realm and its army, she thought. She would destroy the Light itself.

MACKENZIE'S JOURNAL
DAY THIRTEEN

How much of this are my thoughts? How much actually comes from you, God?

The more you listen to my spirit, the more you know my voice. Learn to listen. Learn to trust. I am the lamp for your feet, the light that lights your path. But you must choose to listen, hear and follow the path laid out for you. The journey with me is one of faith. It is simple. The more you trust in my words, the more your faith is active and the more confident you become in believing my words.

I am the Truth and the Life. All truth comes from me. My words are always true. Man has perverted my words, used them for power, to enslave, for self-gain. The evil one tries to change them, cloud their meaning in man's thoughts. You must learn to look past all that man has done, all that man has tried to corrupt and see the truth of my words. Look with no filters of man, but look from your spirit through mine directly into my heart and you will understand that my words are the truth. Remember that I and my words are one and we are at one with the Father, and I wish to be one with my creation.

My spirit earnestly seeks those who are awakened to my presence that is already within man. My breath is your life. Even those who do not know me have my breath of life within them. There are so many who are so close to awakening to my presence. From all backgrounds, all religions, even those who say that I don't exist at all. Even those people are but a breath away from awakening in the spirit to the truth of the kingdom.

My creation yearns for me even if they don't see me. I created man that way, body, soul and spirit, three in one, just as I am. My creation sees me in all that I created, even if they don't believe that I am.

I am the Eternal One. I created you even before the creation of the world as you know it. I sacrificed for you before you were even conceived in my heart. For the Lamb of God was sacrificed even before the foundation of this world. Therefore, I am in all things, even good and bad. All things were created by me and for me.

So even if my people, my most special of all creations, say that I do not exist, I still AM.

I still give all my breath of life. Learn to see my creation the way I see it. See people, all people, no matter what they have done or what they say or what you think about them. See them the way I see them. If you look into a man's eyes, even a man who has not yet awakened to my presence. If you look into a man's eyes in all pureness with no preconceived ideas or opinions. If you look into a man's eyes, any man's eyes and see what I see, you will see me looking back at you. Because I see my creation the way, I created them to be, not what this false world has made them be.

Understand that all sin, all wrath, all death, all decay, all corruption died with me on the cross.

So, look past what is already dead in mankind and see the truth and once you see the truth in someone, then you can awaken their spirit so that they too can see the truth.

Did I not say in my word that I was in prison and you did not visit me, I was hungry and you did not feed me? I was naked, and you did not clothe me. My disciples asked what I meant by this. They said that they had never seen me in any of these conditions. But I was trying to convey this same message. They did not see me looking back at them from the eyes of hurting people all around them.

So now you must learn to see the truth that is behind the lie of the enemy.

The children are playing in the parking lot across the road from you. You see them in their innocence. See me as well. I am with all three of them even if they do not fully understand my presence.

See the potential within all my creation, the destiny and purpose that I have placed in all of men's souls.

Forester, you see the potential of a young forest, one that is overgrown with vines, one where the inferior trees are competing against the trees that you planned to grow. You see the potential and work to bring that potential out.

Do the same with all my creation. Do the same with the gardens in your yard, the forest you work in, the house I have given you, the job you have and the talents I have placed in you. All my creation deserves to grow and bloom and reproduce according to how I intended for them to do.

This is so much truer in my greatest creation, man.

True ministry in the Kingdom of God is not great preaching, marvelous revivals, traveling the world in missions, building great churches for the sake of doing these things. True ministry in my kingdom is to see each man the way I see them, look into to their eyes until you see me looking back and then doing whatever it takes, including all the things I just spoke, until each man is awakened to my presence and understands their true identity in Christ.

Nothing that clouds man's ability to awaken will bind man's soul after man has awakened to my presence.

All things will burn away from man's soul once he has awakened his spirit to my presence. Therefore, I am a consuming fire, not a fire of wrath which has already come to pass, but the fire of purity and love that burns the lies of the enemy that blinds the spirit of man.

CHAPTER TWENTY TWO

The horse ran through the desert through the day and night with the message that her master had tied to the saddle, knowing its importance even though she did not understand what it said. Several times, she saw men on horseback crossing the plains and once they chased her, but she prided herself as the fastest horse in Soteria and knew they could not catch her.

Finally, however, her strength began to fade, her breathing labored, and she desperately needed water, but there was no water to be had. But she knew that she had to get the message to Soteria at all cost, including her own life. The Shadow Realm now depended on her and her alone to get the message to Soteria in time.

So, she continued to run as fast as she could, even though her breathing was labored, and her heart was beating ever quicker to the point of bursting. Pain pulsed through every breath and she began to wobble and had to slow to a walk. She smelled the river with its life-giving water and knew that she was so close, but ever far away.

She had come too far to die just within sight of her goal in a place where the message could not be found and doubled her efforts to run but could no longer do so. She stopped; sweat pouring from her, her breathing loud and labored and her heart racing. She snorted and neighed for help. Surely a guard could hear her, but no one came. The towers overlooking the river crossing were just on the horizon. She could see the torches burning in the night.

She stopped and lowered her head, dizzy and almost to the point of falling, but she had to keep going. She was created for this very moment and knew that it was her job to give everything to get the message through. After a moment, she continued walking toward the tower with its beacon of light, and with her final, last bit of strength, she stumbled up to the crossing and collapsed next to the river.

Carmen climbed the ladder to the top of the tower, replacing the guard who had been at the post for the past few hours. He looked past the red cliffs toward the distant mountain range lost in the shadows of the night, and noticed, for the first time, that they appeared to be closer than he ever remembered. That was odd, he thought. He glanced down below him to the river and saw the horse fall. For a moment, he wondered what he had seen and then noticed the horse appeared to be saddled. He could not see any rider. Carmen immediately rang the tower bell and climbed quickly back down the ladder.

Several others were at the horse when Carmen ran up to the animal. He immediately recognized the horse to be Jonathan's. The horse lay on her side, her head back, and her eyes wide open. Her breathing strained as she raised her head a bit and then let it fall again as Carmen knelt beside her.

"Easy girl. You're okay," Carmen said, not really believing what he had said.

He patted the horse as Heather pushed through the growing crowd to kneel beside the younger man. She gasped when she too recognized the horse.

"What happened?" she asked.

"I don't know Heather. I saw her fall by the river," Carmen answered.

Heather stood up, looking across the river, "Jonathan!" she called and looked down to Carmen, "Did you see anyone?" she asked.

"No, just the horse," Carmen replied.

Peter pushed through the crowd a moment later, "What happened?'

Heather answered him, her worry evident in her answer, "It's Jonathan's mare and she looks like she has run all day. Something must have happened, Peter."

Peter took a step away from the horse and stared into the blackness of the night. Something must have happened. Jonathan could be somewhere out there in the desert in trouble, he thought.

Heather came up beside him and pulled at his arm, "Peter, we have to do something!"

But what could they do? Peter thought.

The horse suddenly raised her head up and to the side, trying to reach to the saddle. Carmen tried to calm her, but she kept trying to pull at the saddle itself until finally, Carmen noticed the note tied to the pommel.

He pulled the note loose and shouted, "Peter! there's a note!"

Carmen took the note and ran over to where Heather and Peter stood. Peter grabbed the note and walked over to one of the torches at the crossing and read it quietly to himself, his face showing no emotion as he read Jonathan's warning. Peter stood for a moment, the news hard to take, but his training and experience had taught him not to overreact to anything, but to take a moment and let the news sink in before taking any type of action.

"Carmen, sound the alarm for the army to assemble," he ordered and handed the note to Heather.

Immediately, all who heard the order rushed back over the crossing to the village and Carmen pulled on the ropes to sound the alarm. Heather stood by the horse, by herself and read the note from Jonathan.

Peter, an army is massing by the river in higher numbers than we ever could imagine. Something is happening in the Shadow Realm. All is changing, but I don't know how to explain it. The Shadow Realm appears to be shrinking, and soon they will be at the crossing. Hold the crossing at all cost. I will return as fast as I can. Jonathan.

Heather crumbled the note in her hand and looked down at the horse. She knelt by the horse and rubbed her neck with sadness. She had given all she had to get the note to them in time. The red cliffs began falling in on themselves, but Heather was not worried or even alarmed by what was happening. The Shadow Realm was indeed shrinking, she thought. She held the Light in her hand and knew with a peace that was beyond all comprehension, that all was well and that with the passing of the Shadow Realm, a new kingdom would emerge.

She rose and walked quickly back across the river. She would face whatever was coming at the side of her mate, the warrior Peter. The Light had given the entire Shadow Realm the ability to fight for her own freedom, she thought. The Light shined brightly with a promise.

MACKENZIE'S JOURNAL
DAY FOURTEEN

Father, sometimes I grow tired......

I know son. I did as well when I walked the earth. I sat very still and listened to the world around me. You do the same. Learn to travel slow when it is time to do so and fast when it is time to travel fast. Like all things, follow me. I will lead you by the still waters. Always rest in me. Spiritual rest. Even on your busiest days when all seems to go wrong, rest in my presence. Remember you are a new creation outside of the bounds of time, even while in time. Learn to rest in my spirit even when going through the hard times. Learn to rest physically as well.

It amazes me how much you don't believe my word. I told my disciples once not to worry. Look at the birds, see how I feed them. Look at the flowers, see how I clothe them. You are my greatest most blessed creation. If I do this for the birds and flowers, how much more do I wish to do for you?

You set and watch the groundhog eat grass in front of you, the squirrels feeding in the trees above you, the birds flying around you. All of them are doing exactly what I created them to do. On this beautiful morning, you see my creation come alive before your eyes. They are totally content with the identity that I gave them. And to do what I created them to do, I give them everything they need.

The same is true with you, but I am saddened that you don't see it. When you have sealed your identity in me and place all of your faith in me, then you too can live your life to the fullest, each of you doing what I created you to do. Fully content in doing and living. And I will give you what you need to do what I have destined for you.

I come to you in many ways, in many forms, in many people. Learn to see me in my creation. Learn to see me in the people all around you. Look at my children until you see me looking back. My children have an identity problem. If you want to spread my kingdom from person to person, then start by finding a person's true identity. Show them that I am already there with them. Allow me to flow from your encounters with me into their soul. Show my love for you, and then they can be awakened to my presence. And then their personal journey of relationship can begin. You are a vessel of my spirit, a habitation for my presence in the earth. A place from where I can overflow like rivers of fresh water. Once you make a personal connection with a person, and see them the way I see them, then a gate can be opened for my spirit to flow from your spirit to theirs. True relationship and fellowship are formed, and their journey can begin as their spirit is awakened by my presence.

Don't be so serious about things. Learn to have fun in the process. I am your Father. I have created a safe place for you to play. Trust in me to show you the boundaries of my safe place and then even when life seems to crash down hard against you, the struggles of life strong, you can still know that as a loving Father, I have a safe place for you. I am in you. You are also in me, hidden in me through Jesus. Therefore you are totally hidden in the safety of my presence.

So live with certain assurance in your identity as my child, knowing that nothing can separate you from my love. No struggle can destroy you, because you are as a child playing in the safety of a father's home. I will always be with you, always protect you, and always love you.

CHAPTER TWENTY THREE

The valley lay hidden under a thick, gray veil of fog, only the tallest rocky pinnacles extending through, the snowbanks glistening in the early morning sun with streaks of pale blue and green fading into creamy white. Lillian stood beneath the shelter of a thickly forested slope by an outcrop of granite that offered her a full view of the great valley below her. The morning air was cold and quiet, the stillness overpowering, lonely.

She had awakened just before daylight, a powdering of light snow covering the heavy bearskin that she used as a blanket. She had lain for a few moments under the warmth of the fur, just her eyes peeking out from under its protection, before finally forcing herself from her haven. Her small fire from the night before was now only a frosty bed of gray ash. With shaking hands, she sifted beneath the ash to the welcome warmth below, found a few tiny blinking embers and placed a hand full of dry grass over them, blowing lightly.

The red embers blinked and then glowed faintly for a few seconds, blinked again and then with a sudden burst of energy ignited the grass. Lillian quickly placed more grass over the small flame and then followed the grass with a few little sticks. The fire gladly embraced the sticks in new life, the orange and red flames quickly consuming the dry fuel. Lillian added more sticks and then larger fuel that she has smartly gathered up the night before and covered with a light blanket to keep them dry overnight.

Lillian had eaten light, just a biscuit and a bit of dried meat, washing the food down with melted snow. She traveled light. The bearskin used as a blanket at night served her well in the mountain cold during the day. The bearskin draped over her shoulders, attached in front with a small leather cord. She also wore a cloak and her own pants and cotton shirt, her other clothes tied in a bundle together with her meager food supply and slung over her back with a small bit of rope.

The sky above was clear, deep blue except for scattered thin clouds painted lavender and pink by the emerging light from a hidden sun. Below her, however, the valley lay hidden beneath the fog. A slight breeze stirred, and the mist responded to its caress, flowing across her. The mist was thick and cold; leaving a film of wetness over her that was almost fine particles of ice. Lillian pulled the bearskin tighter around her. She walked to the very edge of the cliff hanging over the shadows below her.

The mist continued to lift, drawn by the warmth of the sun, but the recesses of the canyon below would remain in the shadows of the great mountain for most of the day. The fog remained entrenched along the narrow canyons, swirling gray and black like a live creature. A narrow trail etched its way down the side of the canyon walls void of trees below the rim where the girl stood. Halfway down the mountain, the slope eased and the trail entered dark pines just above the heavy fog that seemed not to lift at all, but did thin somewhat in places, revealing the tops of giant hemlocks and strange red and blue rock outcrops. At one point far across the valley toward the rising sun, a river sparkled briefly and then just as quickly disappeared behind the gray veil. A sign etched in a deadened tree read, "Valley of Dry Bones."

Lillian stood at the edge of the canyon rim, thinking of all that had happened. She had run through the tunnel, thinking that Jonathan and the servant girl was behind her, but the tunnels had collapsed just as she had exited the doorway. She had waited for most of the day, trying several times to remove the rubble, but to no avail.

She had found herself in a beautiful forest. A trail led away from the doorway through the overhanging limbs. A first, she had been frightened when she had found herself alone once more. Immediately she had felt for the Light around her neck, but it was only a small jewel. This had unnerved her until she realized that somehow in this realm, the Light seemed to be everywhere. And there was a presence all around her that she could vaguely remember from a time before. The presence somehow communicated for her to travel down the trail and find what lay on the other side. After going a short distance, she had found the bearskin and extra clothes, which she had retrieved.

And carved in the rock by the clothes was written.

Surely Goodness and Mercy will follow you all the days of your life and you will dwell in the house of the Lord forever.

What a strange place she had found herself in, she thought. But everything that had happened to her the past few weeks was strange. Why shouldn't this be, she mused. Maybe this was the Kingdom she had seen from the valley before. Maybe she had finally found the way. But then, just as quickly as the thought entered her mind, she knew that this was another place, a half world, a place that led toward the Kingdom, but was not the one she had seen. She smiled and continued down the trail until the night before when she had camped on the mountain rim.

Now, Lillian lowered herself over the lip of the canyon and jumped the few feet to the trail below reluctantly, but she could not go back. Immediately upon landing on the trail below the rim, she felt the oppressive weight of the surrounding mountains. The valley below her seemed full of gloom, dreadful with the slight stench of death floating on the breeze. The last of the mist escaped over the canyon rim, leaving only the thick fog below her along the valley floor.

What sort of place was she descending into? Lillian breathed deeply and fought the urge to turn and climb back up to the forest above, to run from the feeling of oppression that rose from the depths below. But her quest held her firm. She knew that she had to follow the trail to the other side. Below her lay a great valley, a place of mystery, and a place very few people had traveled. She must be crazy, she thought. But a stirring deep within her pulled her ever forward.

At first, the footing was treacherous, the ground a gravelly sand with scattered larger rocks. For several hundred feet the trail descended across the face of the cliff through broken clefts of rock before finally dropping between a crack in the canyon wall and leveling out among a small group of tangled pines that held tenaciously to the thin soil for survival.

The mountain air almost burned with cold and was thin with little oxygen, forcing her to gasp with each breath. Lillian stopped by the pines, breathing deeply, and surveyed the depths below her. Ghostly trees wavered through the thick fog below her as the cloud continued to swirl across the bottom of the valley. Far off to the east, the fog was so thick that it seemed to be a part of the ground itself, a deadened gray landscape except where the red and blue rock spirals jutted upward toward the freedom of the blue sky.

No sound emerged from the valley, no birds called, no animals moved, nothing seemed alive except for the fog itself.

"It's just fog," Lillian whispered, but somehow, she did not quite believe her statement.

She continued along the trail, dropping further down the side of the mountain to a point where she could no longer see across the valley. Immediately below her, individual trees appeared through the veil and then groups of trees, mostly large green-topped pines with occasional oaks void of leaves, white-barked and sickly. The canopy was thick, the understory black as if the cloud prevented any light to penetrate the greenery. As she walked closer to the trees, the fog retreated, fully revealing the first group of trees that grew along the lower slopes.

Her spirits improved as the cloud continued to move back as she neared the edge of the great forest. Hopefully, the oppressive cloud would finally yield to the sun's pull of warmth. The ground here was matted with a thick carpet of needles and spongy moss, the ground wet with patches of snow among the shadows. A stream gurgled merrily somewhere among the trees, the sound a contradiction in the valley where only the fog appeared to have life. Even the trees seemed to be dead.

Lillian noted that usually, places such as this would be teeming with life, but there was nothing. There was no sound except her own breathing and the stream that as she entered the forest disappeared as well.

She walked past the first trees, still on the trail that curved through the forest and disappeared behind the wall of fog. What about this place created such an environment of oppression and despair? The valley had been called the Valley of Bones, but why? What mystery lay hidden within the dark gloom?

The fog churned through the trees several hundred feet within the forest, building itself up into a solid wall that suddenly stopped moving, but continued to pulsate with a constant rhythm as if breathing.

Lillian took a step back. It was only fog pushed by the wind, she thought, but there was no wind. The silence was terribly oppressive, the weight of the mountain overpowering her will to continue. Her mind began to spin in unison with the gathering fog that seemed to draw toward her.

Suddenly, she panicked as the fog jumped forward through the trees and she turned to run back up the trail, but it was gone, replaced by broken rocks and a sheer red cliff wall that began to enclose around her. The air thinned, the silence deadening. She turned frantically searching for a way to escape as the fog climbed outward from the edge of the forest, increasing in height as ghostly images floated within its gray mantle.

The fear was too great, the weight too heavy, the silence too deadly and Lillian fell over backwards, screaming as the cloud rolled over her. She could not hear her own screams.

The gray fog lay heavy upon her back like a cold, soaked blanket that crushed her against the rocky ground with fear. Fear so strong that it clamped strong hands of terror over her heart, binding her lungs so that each breath was labored and painful. She pushed her way from the ground, her heart beating strongly, her sight reduced to just a few feet around her, adding to her fear as she crawled through the gray soup. Shadows swirled through the gray, unrecognizable shadows that appeared to be alive, a part of the fog, but somehow separate.

She had to get up, find the trail and climb back out of the murkiness, but the trail was gone. How could that be? Only the red cliff walls were behind her, but they too were completely hidden by the mantle of fear that engulfed her. Her heart raced unnaturally, her lungs burning as she forced herself to breathe, but the air was dense, acrid and smelled of burning flesh. She closed her eyes, replacing the gray with total black, trying to will her heart to slow, but the black was even more foreboding, so she opened her eyes again, searching. There was only gray, impenetrable living, overpowering gray of fear. It clung to her like a wild animal does its prey, clamping tighter on her chest, the weight unbearable as its death grip tightened over first her chest and then stomach.

Lillian struggled violently, trying desperately to stand, but the weight was too heavy. The fog slithered around her from the waist up to her neck, the crushing weight preventing oxygen from reaching her starved lungs and she began to grow dizzy. She knew that soon she would pass out and be forever drawn into the fog's fearful embrace. But what could she do?

There was nothing to fight. No way to break the hold over her. No one to help her. She was totally alone. She fought to strip the bearskin from her, but it clung to her by an unseen power. She reached outward and felt the cold granite wall and pushed with all of her remaining strength to stand to her feet. She finally pulled her knees under her, and then pulling up against the rocks, she stood. The weight loosened some and she gasped for air, but before she could take a second breath, the fog tightened again.

She was going to die, she thought. She knew that suddenly. The fear was too strong, the emptiness around her too great. With that realization, the weight tightened even more, and she turned her head, reaching for her throat. She felt something cold and scaly, leathery skin around her. Suddenly twin yellow eyes flashed before her out of the fog before her face, and she screamed. This time she could hear it as it echoed off the wall behind her.

"Don't look into the eyes and it will lose strength," a voice shouted from the cliff wall above her.

Lillian wiggled away and took two more breaths before the giant reptile tightened its grip on her again. The fog cleared around her, but the weight remained as the serpent continued to slide its way upward around her neck, the head just above her forehead. Lillian closed her eyes and turned her head away as the serpent lowered its head to face her, the forked tongue licking outward and across her cheek. She felt the tongue tap her lightly, but she continued to keep her eyes closed.

"Hold on girl! If you keep your eyes closed, you have a chance to overcome the spell. Fear is an emotion that we can all control, but we can't fall under its spell," the voice spoke again, this time closer.

Pebbles fell across her head and the serpent hissed. Lillian felt the flicking tongue over her face again and smelled its foul breath of something long dead. But at least she could now breath. Her left arm was bound tightly to her side, but her right was free. She felt down her waist to the knife at her belt, but the bearskin prevented her from reaching the knife at first.

At least now she knew what it was that had attacked her. If she could somehow retrieve her knife, she would kill the serpent. Someone was climbing down the wall toward her, but she had no faith in the man's ability to save her. In fact, he could just be another possible enemy. She finally pulled the knife from the scabbard with some difficulty and slowly raised the knife up to her shoulder. She would open her eyes quickly to locate the head and thrust the knife up through the neck.

"Don't do it," the voice whispered, this time directly beside her.

Lillian wanted to open her eyes, needed to so that she could locate the snake, but the fear was too great. She had one chance.

"Fear waits for you to look into its eyes so that it can rule over you. The knife cannot kill the serpent. But if you look totally away from fear, you will not give it a platform on which to continue to assault your emotions. It will pull back its head and then I can kill it for you."

"How can I trust you, a stranger in this strange place? For all I know you are this creature's master," Lillian spoke to the voice beside her, thinking that the voice seemed familiar somehow.

The voice took on a fatherly tone, "Suit yourself young lady, but what I have said is true. I have seen many who have come this way who have never left. They wonder forever in the fog that is fear. But you are different. Now lower the knife, pull your head back and to the side and hold completely still. I can save you if you do as I say."

The tongue flicked her again on the lips and Lillian pulled back in disgust and turned her head toward the voice. She opened her eyes. The fog swirled around her, finally lifting toward the sun. A man stood next to her; half hidden by the mist itself. He was not much taller than herself. He had curly black hair, a short beard, and mustache; the beard flecked with gray. The man was dressed as a woodsman with brown cotton pants and a dark green shirt. He wore high black boots and a green overcoat that hung down below his knees. A glint of steel glistened in the morning rays of the sun that moved across the valley floor, reflecting against the fog and giving life to the red and blue spirals.

The snake's embrace tightened, and she shrieked in pain, gasping for air. The yellow eyes appeared again before her, but she turned away just as a brilliant flash of steel arched through the mist, slicing through the snake's head, splitting the eyes and immediately the snake disappeared back into the fog that had spawned it.

Lillian fell to her knees, gasping and coughing, clutching her throat with both hands. The man knelt beside her and placed his hands on her shoulders. Instinctively Lillian backed away, glaring at the man defensively, but then calmed herself. He had saved her life, she thought. But he was a stranger and all that was within her told her to beware.

The man had dark brown eyes that were partially hidden by unruly locks of curly black hair.

"Thank you, sir," she managed to say as he helped her to her feet, "Thank you for killing that thing."

The man sheathed his sword, the blade immediately hidden beneath the great overcoat. The fog swirled behind him, gathering itself among the trees and pulled back into the shadows of the forest where it lay along the ground as if wounded. Lillian shuttered. The fog was a living, breathing organism, one that had almost killed her.

The man pointed at the fog, "Fear lies around us all the time in this life, fear and its companion, worry. We fear what we do not understand. We worry about things that we have no control over or that may never happen. But both can be overcome as long as we don't give them the power. When they materialize before us, we must not look into their eyes. We must look past them to see our salvation. In fact, at times we must completely turn away from their form and they will retreat into the mist. See the fog is thinning. You can walk through it now because it has lost its power over you."

The low fog was breaking up, scattering and revealing the patches of snow, rotting logs and something bleached white that lay scattered far into the forest. What was that? Lillian thought.

"But will it come back. I could not kill it. You said that yourself. What will I do if it returns? I have far to travel across the valley."

The man thought for a moment, eyeing the girl before him, "You are a strong one girl. I can tell that. I think that once you see your power over something, you will be able to continue to overcome it. Give yourself more credit. In this valley, fear always slinks in the corners, waiting for a chance to attack again, but you will be ready next time."

Lillian shook her head, "You give me too much credit sir."

"Besides dear lady. I must also travel across the valley for a time. I know the ancient paths. If you wish we could travel together. I may be able to help you."

"You have traveled this place before?" Lillian asked.

The thought of proceeding deeper into the gloom of the forest left her ill at ease, although her fear of the canyon had subsided greatly. The towering rock walls did not seem to bear down upon her so much as when she first began her descent down the narrow trail to the bottom.

But before her lay an endless forest of dark trees and even darker shadows plus the ever-present fog. Even as she stood before the strange man, the fog swirled along the forest floor, gathering in rocky enclaves or up against the base of the larger pines, breathing and pulsating with a life of its own.

The man seemed not to notice, "Yes, yes dear girl. I know the valley well. In fact, I know the land of forest and mountains from the gates of the ocean to storehouses of King Elohim himself. I am one of the King's foresters, keeper of his vast estates. Please forgive my rudeness. In the excitement, I failed to introduce myself."

The forester stood straighter than before, standing as tall as he could and then bowed deeply before Lillian, as she stood embarrassed at his chivalry.

"My name is Eleos, at your service."

Lillian flushed as the forester took her gloved hand in his and kissed the top of her hand lightly before standing back up, his eyes sparkling brightly in the light. He looked familiar somehow, but she could not place from where. He had saved her life, and if he truly was who he said that he was, then he could lead her through the forest safely to the other side.

"I am Lillian from…" she thought of her home, of the Shadow Realm, of Jonathan who was somewhere on the other side, or was he? "Just Lillian. Thank you, sir, for saving me. Thank you for helping me. This forest of shadows does frighten me, and I am glad that I don't have to travel through it alone."

Eleos shook his head, glancing at the fog, a gray veil that covered the ground again. The leading edges flowed past them like water, hiding their feet beneath its blanket. Lillian backed up nervously, but it now appeared to be harmless.

"Don't worry Lillian. You have overcome the fear of it. The fog has no power over you unless you give it power."

"What is it? How can it be alive?"

Eleos had no answer but only shook his head.

"There are many things within this valley that I do not understand. They are from the ancient past; this I do know. But why Elohim placed them here, I cannot tell you. Don't worry. I will lead you through, but I can only do so much to help you. You must overcome the challenges before you as well."

MACKENZIE'S JOURNAL DAY FIFTHTEEN

We have to be about the Father's business. What is that, you say?

God, what is the answer?

Reveal the Son to the world. Reveal my love for my creation. Open a gateway to the hearts of man where I can flow from heaven to earth. See my creation the way I see it. Show my love for all man through your actions and words that I give you. Follow my example. Learn to trust my spirit, my voice in the innermost recesses of your mind.

Be the light when there is no light anywhere to be found. Go into all situations in the full assurance of who I made you to be. Enjoy the experience of my spirit working within you. Lust for the passion that comes from my presence flowing through you and in you. Feel the power and love, joy, peace, and righteousness that I give you.

The more you become a gateway touching the throne, the more of my presence you will feel and the more my spirit can flow into all those around you. Then you will begin to see people come to you to ask about me. Because as I am lifted up, I will draw all men unto me.

I will open, you, a window to heaven and all that is me will flow through that window.

But you must be true to yourself. You must know your true identity. You must know the name that I have called you and the words I have spoken over you from the foundation of the world. When you were hidden in the secret places, I knew you. I breathed my life into you, and you were even then in my presence.

Don't let the false lights of this present age blind you to the true Light of the World. Remember my presence when you were hidden in your mother's womb or even before. Because I have known you even before.

You can hear my first voice, the first time I spoke over you. At the moment of your conception, when I breathed my life's breath into you, your spirit came alive and you saw me, heard my voice, fellowshipped in my love for you.

CHAPTER TWENTY FOUR

The army of Soteria gathered by the river crossing as ordered, thousands of past fugitives who were as much a part of the Shadow Realm as the Shadow Realm itself, now free of their chains and empowered by strength not of their own to defend themselves. The rules had changed once the Apostolos Or had defeated Krino and activated the Light within the Shadow Realm. Malak and Nasar, the two Ben Elohim, had once had an active role in the Shadow Realm, but they left to go to other realms where their services were needed.

In the old world, the Shadow Realm had been ruled over by mighty Archons and the Shadow Realm fought among itself. The Light had always been present in one form or another since the Shadow Realm had been created, and there had been those who had gained an understanding of its power, but the Apostolos Or himself was the one that had to activate it totally within the realm.

Peter stood in the guard tower searching the plains across the horizon for any sign of the attacking army that Jonathan had warned of. The red cliffs across the river had fallen in on themselves. The mountains and great forest had disappeared next and now only the vast Plains of Apistia spread outward away from the river to vanish at the horizon. Peter noted that whatever was happening, it seemed not to have affected Soteria itself, only the land across the river.

Heather climbed the ladder and joined her partner in the tower overlooking the river crossing. She was dressed in armor and held a shield and sword. Her long, braided hair spiraled in a circle behind her head, tied with purple ribbons. Peter glanced down, noticed her hair and smiled.

"I like what you did with your hair," he remarked.

"Thank you, love. I figured if this was to be our last time together in this realm, I wished to look remarkable," she teased, and laughed, touching her hair and smiled brightly, "Plus, it gets in the way otherwise."

Peter squeezed her hand and kissed the top of her forehead, "Are they ready?" he asked.

"One half is on guard like you requested and the other half is resting. In a few hours, they will switch." Heather answered.

"Good, so we wait," Peter spoke calmly. He had come to terms with himself that if the enemy attacked, his forces would probably not be able to hold the crossing for long, but they would hold it at all cost. That was all they could do. He knew that they had to hold out until Jonathan arrived with Lillian. That was their only true chance, he now knew.

The two watched as workers finished the heavy gates below them. Two gates had been constructed, one on each side of the river. Peter had placed the best archers in the forward towers along with swordsmen. He had fortified the gates and added large barrels of oil that could be used to pour fire down on any troops that tried to scale the tower walls. On the other side of the river, the same had been done. Each tower was connected by a bridge that if the front defenses were overran, could be used for escape across the bridges and then destroyed afterward. On the Soteria side of the river, further fortifications had been constructed that were also filled with archers who could cover the approaches to the crossing. Standing in the crossing itself were shield baring soldiers with pikes and swords that would defend the crossing.

The only place to cross the river was at the crossing, which was approximately 100 feet wide. If the first gate was broken, the attackers would face a solid wall of shields and pikes that they would have to defeat before they could gain access to the second wall. Also, several large catapults had been constructed and placed behind the second wall that would fire burning missiles over the front wall into the attacking army.

It was a good defensive plan, Peter thought, but he also knew the resolve of the enemy. They would throw their lives away easily to do the bidding of the Archons out of fear more than loyalty. He, on the other hand, valued every warrior under his command. They were all willing to die to save Soteria, but hopefully, they would not have to. However, he knew that it was only a matter of time before he would run out of soldiers to defend the crossing and then all would be lost.

His thoughts were interrupted as Carmen climbed into the tower, "Peter, the gate is complete. Do you wish us to close it for good?" he asked.

Peter thought for a moment. When they closed the gates, they could not be opened very easily again. Although there had only been a few fugitives who had stumbled in the last few days, there was a chance there could still be others out there.

"No, wait until the very last moment, Carmen. There may yet be fugitives that need to get in," he ordered. He knew it was a chance to leave the gate open any longer, but he would not close the gate until he was sure that all the fugitives had gained safety over the river.

The warrior Nathan entered the tower as Carmen left. He had been in Soteria when Peter and Heather had first arrived and had rushed forward on horseback to fight the approaching Knights of Krato.

"Peter, I have thirty horsemen ready at the crossing, but I don't think we will be useful on horseback. We will take the front at the crossing on foot," he stated.

Peter looked down at the crossing and saw the armored Soteria knights standing in rank beside their mounts. They were the best soldiers he had with the most training. He thought for a moment before concluding that he could not have them in the front ranks. He would place them at the second wall, as the last-ditch defense. Or if by some miracle, the enemy's attack was shattered, he would use them to rush forward on horseback and destroy whatever enemy was left.

Peter shared the strategy with Nathan, and although displeased by the decision at first, Nathan understood the logic behind the tactic.

"Very well Peter. I will station them at the second wall." Nathan responded.

"Thank you, Nathan," Peter thanked him as Nathan turned to leave, "Wait, Nathan, keep a third on station at all times at the first gate while the gate remains open just in case."

"Yes sir," Nathan responded with a smile. He would be at the first gate the entire time until the gate shut, he thought.

Peter turned and set against the back wall of the tower and motioned for Heather to set beside him. Lookouts watched from each tower with orders to sound the alarm if they saw anything.

Heather set back against the wall beside him and leaned her head on his chest as he placed his arm around her. They were both tired and needed to sleep, if not for just for a little while.

Peter's deep sleep was suddenly interrupted by someone shaking him.

"Peter, people are coming! Shall I sound the alarm" the guard exclaimed, overly nervous to the point of panic.

Peter jumped quickly up, causing Heather to fall back against the wall, which awakened her as well. He first reached to help her up and then rushed over to the battlements to gaze out over the plains. The sun was setting over the vastness. He must have slept for several hours, he thought. He looked through the telescope given to him by the guard and immediately saw dozens of people running toward the crossing. They were fugitives, he thought. He looked further back and saw horsemen riding after them and knew immediately that the fugitives would not reach the river in time.

"Signal the archers!" Peter ordered and the guard rang the bell once and then twice more, which was the signal for archers to man the battlements. Immediately archers filled each of the towers and battlements along the river. They were armed with longbows that could reach far out in the plains over the river.

Peter then leaned over the wall and motioned for Nathan, who stood by the open gate with ten horsemen at the ready.

"Nathan, fugitives are coming but there are horsemen behind them. They will never make it. Take your troop out and bring them all in. The archers will try to cover you as best they can. And Nathan, make sure you all come back as well." Peter ordered.

Nathan saluted and turned to the rider next to him who blew from a horn and suddenly the rest of the horsemen galloped across the river crossing. Peter looked back through the telescope. He counted at least thirty fugitives running toward the gate and gaining ground quickly behind them were at least as many mounted soldiers. From their garments, they looked to be a detachment of Kratos knights, the very band he had been in long before.

Peter lowered the telescope and backed away as Heather came up to him. She could see the dread in his eyes.

"What is it?" she asked.

"Kratos," Peter said and they both knew the horror that awaited them if the Kratos knights gained access to the crossing.

They were ruthless killers, well trained and a formable enemy. At one time, they ruled over much of the Shadow Realm under Archon Krino along with the Sahat riders, but they had disappeared after the Apostolos Or had defeated Archon Krino, until now. Peter had once ridden with them until the Light had changed him forever. They were a very bad element of the Shadow Realm that had to be defeated, once and for all.

Heather took the telescope and looked through it. The horsemen were definitely Kratos warriors. She shuttered at the thought of their evil and gave the telescope back to Peter. Jonathan, you need to get back with Lillian quickly, she pleaded. She held the Light in her hands and felt its reassuring warmth.

Thirty horsemen loudly galloped beneath the tower and out across the plains and Peter watched with satisfaction as they formed a V-shaped wedge with Nathan riding in front. The archer captain raised his arm and waited until the enemy were within range. He would have time for one volley before the Soterian knights would ride too close. Peter watched the drama unfold beneath him. As if on cue, Nathan slowed his wedge of riders just as they reached the escaping fugitives and the archer captain lowered his arm. Whistling arrows suddenly rushed overhead and arced toward the attacking Kratos warriors. Peter could see over a hundred now. Too many Nathan! he thought but could do nothing to warn them now.

The range was still too great and many of the arrows fell harmlessly in front of the soldiers, but Peter saw a dozen or so soldiers and horses suddenly fall among the charging horses and a trumpet blew, and Nathan spurred his warriors on. The arrows slowed the attacking Kratos warriors just as the Soterian knights crashed into their ranks. Even from this distance, Peter could hear the sounds of battle. Horses and men screaming, metal clashing against metal, the sickening sounds of swords slashing through bodies, the echo of pain and death. The battle raised such a dust storm that Peter could no longer see but shadows of horsemen fighting under a darkening sky. He watched as the last of the fugitives finally made their way across the river and the guard rang the tower bells as hard and loud as he could.

The Soterian knights suddenly disengaged and fought their way back through the scattered Kratos warriors who charged after them. The archer captain once again lowered his arm and arrows shot forward to cover the retreat. The Kratos knights reined in their mounts just in time and only a few fell to the shower of arrows.

Peter rushed down the ladder and ran over to the river crossing. Some of the villagers were escorting the fugitives back across the river to safety. They were men, women and a few children. One of the women came up to Peter and hugged him.

"Thank you, good sir, you have saved us," she cried.

"Are there any more of you out there?" Peter asked, but the woman did not know.

Peter looked closer at the group and realized that they were not fugitives, they were nomads.

Peter motioned for one of the villagers, "Feed them and cloth them and put them in the council house, but place a guard on them just in case," he ordered.

Nathan rode up and dismounted, "Did they all make it?"

"Yes, and you did great," Peter exclaimed as he watched the horsemen ride past, counting twenty-nine horsemen with only a few wounded. The first round had been to Soteria, he thought and motioned for Carmen to close the gate.

Heather watched from the tower at the sunset with a blaze of red fire on the horizon. She thought she could see dust clouds approaching. Jonathan, where are you? She asked. The Light gave her warmth, but no answer.

CHAPTER TWENTY FIVE

Eleos built a small fire against a granite overhang of rock hidden under a thick canopy of hemlock. A thick mat of hemlock needles covered the ground except where he had scraped them away before placing a ring of rocks to contain the small blaze. The rock overhang offered shelter from the misting, cold rain that fell, the thick hemlock a wall that surrounded the small camp except where he had cut his way to the rock cliff. After helping Lillian through the tangled undergrowth, he had placed hemlock and laurel limbs across the opening to close them in. Lillian did not seem to notice the uncharacteristic nervousness of Eleos as he sat back against the wall and watched the small fire blaze.

Something about the night bothered him, maybe even scared him, if he let fear have a foothold. He had traveled through the valley many times before, but very rarely at night. Something unnatural wandered this night. He had sensed a change in the atmosphere earlier in the day as he and Lillian followed the forest trail. And then the girl had started coughing. Her progress slowed as she became weaker. She had faltered once on the trail, and when he had caught her by the arm to help her over the log, he felt the fever.

Now she sat against the wall by the fire shivering even under the thick bearskin that she used as a covering. Eleos gathered more wood to place by the fire, added a few sticks and then immediately wished he had not done so as the fire brightened significantly. He looked out into the tangled brush and the blackness beyond, hoping that the thick hemlock would hide the fire's glow.

Eleos retrieved a small pot from his pack and placed it on a flat rock that he had situated over the burning coals to form a small oven and poured a small amount of water from his canteen. He then retrieved a leather bag from the pack as well and placed a few leaves into the water, adding several others as he found them in the bag to make a hot tea.

The forest that he had lived in for his entire life offered everything that a person needed if one knew where to look. Food and medicine, weapons and shelter, peace and comfort, even death and destruction, all could be found. The tea would help the fever.

After the tea boiled until the water turned a deep red, Eleos poured the mixture into a cup throwing the leaves themselves out. They were poisonous if swallowed, but the mixture was not. The sweet berry leaf produced a pungent aroma, the tea very strong, but sweet as well.

"Here Mistress Lillian. Drink this." He placed the cup to her lips, and at first, she drew away. The fever burned within her and her face was flushed and red. She opened her eyes and for a moment recognized him. She took the cup then and drank the contents slowly and then suddenly dropped the cup and fell over unconscious.

Eleos placed her close to the fire and retrieved the cup. The sweet berry leaf was very strong but would help reduce the fever as she slept. He had never seen someone get the fever so quickly. The attack of the snake had been the day before. He had hoped that he had saved her in time before the snake had bitten her, but apparently it had infected her somehow, and it had taken a full day for the fever to set in. They had traveled the first day through the valley with no problems, stopping only long enough to eat once and had camped by the river. This day, however, had been completely different. Lillian grew weaker as the day progressed and the forest had changed somehow. Someone or something was following them.

Eleos ate a biscuit and piece of dried beef and allowed the fire to burn itself down even though the night was chilly. The rain had stopped. The rock overhang blocked even the full moon's light and as the fire burned lower, the blackness of the night crept closer.

Eleos awoke suddenly with a jerk of his head. What sound in the night had awakened him? The fire still burned so he could not have been asleep too long. He reached over and placed a hand on the girl's forehead. The fever had subsided, so the tea was working.

A small pebble suddenly fell from the overhang above and into the fire, scattering sparks. Eleos froze and glanced upward. There was nothing there that he could see, but something had moved among the rocks. He slowly backed up against the rock wall deeper under the overhang and drew his sword from the scabbard.

He could see nothing past the pale glow of the fire but only tangled brush and blackness.

And then he saw two yellow eyes staring at him from behind the first row of hemlocks. He glanced over at Lillian. She still slept. It took several hours for the effects of the tea to fade away. He looked back and saw two more sets of yellow eyes staring at him.

Whatever had been following them was here, just past the wall of hemlock.

"We want the girl, Eleos. You stand down. We mean you no harm." A voice growled from the dark.

Eleos grasped the sword tightly and stepped closer to the sleeping girl. She stirred beneath the bearskin.

"You have no rights in this place, Wraith. You can make no demands. I am a Guardian, and these forests are under my rule. So be gone. Leave us be." Eleos demanded.

The voice laughed. "Your forests are full of bones is it not? Bones of fallen warriors from ancient times, bones that your king abandoned here in this place. Just like you."

The Wraith spoke of the Valley of Dry Bones that lay nearby within the forest. Thousands of bones lay scattered across the valley floor, bleached white and shining beneath the sun. They had lain there from time immortal, never touched by human or animal, never decaying. No one knew who they had been, why they were there, what their purpose was. Like many oddities in this land, Eleos accepted them for what they were, a relic of the past that the King had said to leave alone. He had walked the trails past the valley, had seen the bones shining in the sun, but had never ventured into the canyon itself. It was a sacred place. A burial ground that would one day reveal its purpose when the time was right when the creation was fully restored.

"You speak of the Valley of Dry Bones, Wraith. "

Lillian stirred again and moaned. She was waking up. Eleos knew that he would have no choice but to fight to protect the girl. There was no place to run, no place in the darkness to go.

"The valley has no relevance now. You have trespassed on the king's forest, and you must go."

Several voices laughed in unison. The tangled brush moved, branches snapped, and a hooded figure emerged from the hemlock and stood across the fire from Eleos. The wraith stood over six feet. Yellow eyes glowed from beneath the hood.

"You are wrong Eleos. We have not trespassed. We were here long before you came to this forest. My king has not abandoned me like yours. Now I say again, give us the girl, and you may live. Otherwise. I will add your body to the pile of bones."

Gravel fell from the rock ledge, spraying Eleos with pebbles. He stepped back just as another wraith dropped down from the overhang just behind him. A massive club swung outward from the shadow and Eleos ducked and parried the blow with his sword. Lillian screamed behind him as other shadows suddenly sprang from the forest and the hooded figure stepped across the fire now holding a claymore twice the size of Eleos's sword.

Lillian stood up suddenly and fell back against the rock wall. She was fully awake now. The fever was gone because of the medicinal tea, but she was still disoriented. Eleos stood before her. He slashed with his sword, and the first dark figure fell in a heap of clothing and scattered bones. A second jumped at him and dropped as well, and a third ran past Eleos and jumped across the fire, knocking Lillian back against the brush as she managed to draw her knife.

The claymore slashed across the fire which had spread into the dry bed of needles, illuminating the campsite with orange light. Sparks cascaded downward as the two blades met and Eleos buckled under the heavy blow. The wraith howled with bloodlust and drove forward with his large sword. Eleos stood firm and parried the blow again, sidestepped and raked the wraith's abdomen. To his surprise, the blade did not penetrate flesh but scraped against bone.

In a panic, Lillian slashed upward into the dark figure as it fell on her. Her blade lodged between exposed ribs. She kicked viciously outward, knocking the creature back against the rocks where it fell apart, the cloak dropping into the fire, bones scattering over the rocks. She backed away and fell again back into the heavy brush. She saw Eleos parry the blow from the monstrous figure by the fire. She scrambled back toward him out of the brush when, to her horror, the bones that had scattered before her began to quiver and move, one toward another, connecting themselves until a full skeleton with glowing yellow eyes stood before her. The skeleton reached down and picked up the burning cloak and placed it over him and drew from the cloak a sword. The other two that had fallen before stood next to the burning one.

"Get the girl!" screamed the hooded wraith

Lillian fell back into the brush, her fear overtaking her. She had to run.

Eleos stepped back again from the claymore, the rock wall saving him from losing his head. The blade shattered the granite, splitting a section of rock that crashed down around his feet. He jumped through the spreading fire and turned to block another heavy blow.

What monster was this creature, Eleos thought? What horror had awakened in this place? He prayed for the King's protection. He did not fear his own death, but he did fear what they would do to the girl. Lillian scrambled in the brush behind him as three cloaked skeletons fought through the brush after her, one fully on fire now.

His attacker suddenly stopped just across the fire from him, holding the claymore in front of him with the point into the ground. The fire spread around his feet.

"Why do you fight Eleos? I only want the girl."

"Why?" Eleos asked.

"Because she has the power to destroy us all." He answered and jumped across the fire just as the burning skeleton suddenly exploded in the brush.

Lillian finally managed to free herself from the tangled hemlock thicket and emerged into the open forest meadow, the full moon's light glowing across the landscape. It was as light as the morning. The fire glowed from behind the brush, and she saw Eleos' shadow, his blade swinging into... into nothing. There was nothing else.

Three figures emerged from the brush, yellow eyes scanning the forests and she ran.

Eleos fell backward as the skeleton exploded. The claymore slashed downward toward him. He blocked the blow, the force knocking his own sword to the ground and he fell forward. He scrambled around expecting another final killing blow, but only a dark cloak floated downward across him. It smelled of death and decay, and Eleos quickly threw it off him and into the fire. He stumbled back against the wall searching for his assailant, but there was nothing. Only the fire and his pack, the bearskin and Lillian's pack.

And then the bearskin moved, and a girl's hand emerged from beneath the heavy fur and pushed the skin back from her head. Lillian lay sleeping. Eleos stared unbelievingly at the girl still holding his sword. What had happened? It must have been a dream. The fire burned low; the pot of water still sat on the rock where he had left it after giving Lillian the tea. Eleos sat down by the fire, shaking. What a terrible dream. What magic was at work here?

CHAPTER TWENTY SIX

Finally, after several hours, the morning did come to Eleos. And with it came a bright blue sky and glistening rays of sunshine through the hemlock thicket and a throbbing headache from lack of sleep. Eleos added a few sticks to the fire and began preparing coffee. Lillian still slept soundly, and after touching her forehead, he was reassured by a total absence of any fever. Just before the coffee came to a full boil, he removed the pot from the fire and poured himself a cup. The coffee was black and very strong, just the way he liked it.

He sat on the rock used as a chair and leaned back against the wall of the cave, sipping the hot liquid and wondering again what nightmare had occurred the night before. There appeared to be no evidence of any struggle, but he vividly remembered every detail of the encounter. He took another long drink. The coffee was already helping the headache, and studied the girl more closely. She lay on her side, her hands under her small face streaked with ash from the fire. Her breathing was soft and steady. She stirred a bit and then opened her eyes. For the first time, he noticed that they were a deep blue. He had thought that they had been green.

She smiled at him, a smile of someone who had a full assurance that she was in a safe place, a smile of someone who had slept well through the night.

"Good morning Mistress Lillian. Would you like some coffee?"

Lillian sat up and pulled the bearskin from her, stretching as she did so.

"Yes, thank you."

Eleos took a second tin cup from his pack and poured a cup for her, handing it over the small fire to her outstretched hand. She took a sip and grimaced at the strength.

Eleos noticed and laughed, "I'm sorry Mistress. I have always liked my coffee very strong. None of the others were ever able to drink it either. Let me weaken that for you, and I may have a bit of honey in my pack if you would like."

"No, that's okay. This is fine, really," she answered and took another drink.

Lillian looked around her, puzzled, " Where are we, I don't remember. Did I pass out or something?"

"You must have been infected by the snake and ran a high fever. I carried you here and gave you a bit of herbal medicine for the fever. You have been out for almost an entire day and night." Eleos did not say anything about the strange night. That had to have been nightmare, maybe caused by the serpent, he thought.

Lillian noticed her soot-stained hands, "Is there a place somewhere I can freshen up. I feel like I slept in the fire last night."

"Yes of course. There is a stream just below us," Eleos answered as he set the cup down and walked over to the edge of the rock overhang and pulled back the brush he placed the night before.

"And while you are doing that, I will cook us a bit of breakfast. I believe I still have a couple of eggs somewhere in that pack of mine."

Lillian pulled the bearskin tight around her and gingerly stepped over the fire and through the opening in the brush into the strengthening morning sunshine. A merry stream sparkled in the light below the camp a few yards among a tumble of large boulders, the water cascading over a series of small falls before falling into a deeper pool where the water slowed. A few fish lazily floated in the pool, darting quickly back into the shade of the bank as Lillian stepped nearby.

Eleos turned his back respectfully to give the woman privacy and began to prepare the simple breakfast when he suddenly froze.

Something was wrong!

A deep foreboding dread washed over his consciousness warning that things were not what they appeared to be. He glanced back to where the girl washed in the stream. Rays of sunshine penetrated the forest canopy around her, shafts of light shining brightly mixed with morning fog. Beyond her lay the Valley of Bones filled with white bones, long dead. Even then in the morning light, he saw the bones sleeping across the forested meadow as he had seen countless times before. But now they seemed not to be so innocent, especially after the nightmare of the night before.

That was no nightmare! A voice spoke directly to him.

Eleos took hold of his sword and stepped toward the opening.

"Mistress," he called, but there was no answer. He heard the girl splashing in the water and saw a figure through the underbrush by the stream.

This is an illusion! The voice spoke. The girl is in danger!

But she was right there not thirty feet from him washing in the stream, he reasoned.

He took another step and could now see clearly to the stream where the girl stood knee deep in the water, the bearskin now over her head. That was strange, he thought.

"Mistress Lillian," he called again, and the figure turned to face him.

It is an illusion! You are in danger Eleos! The voice called from across the valley, and Eleos stepped back in horror.

Before him stood the wraith from his nightmare. The sunshine vanished as darkness suddenly fell over the valley. The fire shot skyward and bones cracked in the blackness beyond the fire's light. Piercing yellow eyes appeared to be everywhere around him, darting just outside the brush barrier.

Fear! the dread of horrors unknown to humankind. Eleos stepped back over the fire. The bearskin lay where Lillian had slept. The tin cup he had given her just moments before rolled across the hard ground. The forest beyond the firelight echoed with laughter. Eleos had never known such fear, such dread, and such despair.

Get a hold of yourself, Eleos reasoned. The snake must have somehow affected him, he thought. This has to be a dream, a hallucination. This could not be real.

"Oh, this is very real, Eleos" a voice spoke from the darkness and a wraith suddenly appeared in the opening across the fire from where Eleos stood.

Eleos grabbed his broadsword just as the wraith stepped over the fire, swinging a sword down out of the darkness.

A woman screamed somewhere nearby! In desperation, Eleos rushed forward under the swinging blade into the fire itself, the flames scattered beneath his feet, and drove his sword forward and upward through the wraith's midsection. He was surprised that this time, however, the wraith was not a skeleton as before, but was flesh and blood. Blood gushed outward, spilling across his chest and the wraith suddenly screamed in pain like a wild animal wounded.

The wraith fell backward into the brush, pulling Eleos down as well. Eleos fell over the wraith's dying body, holding the sword with both hands, the bearskin falling away. To his horror, he looked into the eyes of a young woman, her face twisted in pain and fear, coughing up blood and gasping for air. Eleos pushed himself away in horror at what he had done. Lillian lay beside him, the sword protruding from her midsection.

Eleos looked wildly around him! His job was to protect the girl! How could such a horrible thing happen? And then he heard a women's soft laughter somewhere out in the shadows of the forest among the bleached bones. He had listened to that laughter many times before and understood who he had been fighting the whole time. Not all was what it appeared to be?

CHAPTER TWENTY SEVEN

Peter stood on the ramparts overlooking the vastness of the Plains of Apistia. However, the night was totally dark, and he could see nothing past the torches by the gates below. He could not sleep, knowing that when the sun rose behind him, the light would reveal what the blackness most likely hid. Peter crept to the other side of the tower where the guard stood vigilant beside the bell. He was young and nervous, having never experienced combat. Peter gave him a reassuring smile and returned to his first position by the wall. Heather lay next to where he stood, asleep. Peter looked down and could barely make out her small face in the low torchlight. She slept peacefully, he thought.

He stood and waited for the sun to rise, which could not be too long, he thought. It had been a full day and night since the first fight by the gate, and only the small band of Kratos knights had stood just outside of arrow range, waiting for the same thing that he waited for. The approach of the army.

Below him, he heard the stirring of a camp awaking. The cooks would stir first, he thought, to start cooking and warming fires, and then soon his own army would come alive with a new day.

Heather stirred below him, and Peter smiled at her as she stretched her small hands outward and yawned. Behind him, the low mountains of Soteria suddenly lightened up with a pale blue light as the sun approached the far horizon. Peter bent down and helped Heather up.

"Good morning, sleepyhead," he said.

Heather yawned again and straightened her back, "Oh my, remind me not to sleep on that hard floor again."

Peter laughed and kissed her on the forehead. "The sun's almost up," she stated.

They both looked as the first sliver of molten orange appeared just over the low forested mountains, revealing a full blue sky, both cloudless and eternal. The shadows retreated across the forest as the sun rose until the tower itself was bathed in the orange glow. Below the tower and across the river, both Peter and Heather saw the entire Soterian army staring toward the west that still lay in the shadows, watching for what they dreaded to be there.

From their perch in the forward tower, Peter and Heather saw the sun's light reveal the river itself far below them and then the sandy shoreline. The moving light then revealed the Kratos knights standing guard by their horses immediately in front of the gate itself. The light mowed back away from the river and flooded the entire plains with a pale glow as the rising sun gained strength.

Peter fully expected to see a vast army on the plains, but behind the row of standing knights, there sat one armored warrior on a horse. Heather pointed further back, and the sun revealed red dust that covered the entire horizon. A dust storm caused by an approaching army, Peter thought.

Peter took the telescope and zoomed into the single warrior that sat upon the horse further back against the desert. The warrior was fully armored in bronze and carried a shield in one hand and a lance in the other. Flying from the lance fluttered a black banner. The warrior took the lance and thrust it into the ground beside him as the black horse reared up, his red eyes glowing fiercely. The banner was black with a red dragon on both sides

The horse snorted and reared again, and then sidestepped and pranced as the warrior stared up at the tower. The man had long black hair and a full beard and Peter immediately recognized him as Archon Planos. The warrior spurred his horse up to the Kratos knights and stopped just in front of their sentry line. The death horse stood still, his glaring eyes probing the gate itself with red beams of light.

The warrior shouted," I am Archon Planos. My army is approaching. Your only hope is to open the gates now and allow me to enter. Otherwise, I will show no mercy. Your Apostolos Or and his harlot have abandoned you. The Shadow Realm will die. You will all die unless you open the gates now and allow me entrance. This is your only chance to live."

In the tower, Peter motioned for the guard to give him a longbow. He took an arrow and dipped it in the barrel of oil and then set it on fire. He pulled back as far as he could and fired. The arrow arced high in the air and then ascended with a whistle, the fire trailing like a comet, and struck the sandy beach only a few feet in front of Planos. A great, defiant cheer rose up from the warriors who manned the walls and saw the arrow strike.

"Well, that should do it," Peter said as he handed the bow back to the guard, "Sound the alarm."

Planos stood silently, watching the arrow burn out in front of him and then turned his horse and rode back to the sentry line where another warrior stood, holding a large trumpet. Just as the tower bells of Soteria rang, the warrior blew from the trumpet, and suddenly the dust cloud on the horizon materialized into a massive army of warriors, marching shoulder to shoulder for as far as one could see.

Heather gasped at the sight emerging from the dust cloud on the horizon. Peter clasped her hand in his as she grabbed the Light around her neck. Peter watched with an experienced warrior's eyes at the approaching army, trying to determine the type of forces arrayed against him.

The first troop was led by a giant riding a chariot that wore no armor and held only a giant club. Long hair covered his body, and his face and shoulders were painted with bright red paint. A thousand warriors, all naked but for a loincloth and covered in hair and painted red and blue followed this leader. Peter knew them to be the dreaded Harag. They massed to one side of the line of Kratos knights and screamed a bloodthirsty shout as they stopped at their assigned position.

Peter watched as the second troop of thousands of bronze warriors emerged from the red dust cloud on the horizon. Their leader rode a gray horse with the red eyes of a death horse. The warrior was armored in full body armor that shone brightly in the morning sun. Long, blond hair flowed down his back, and he had the face of a young boy, although he was a full-grown man, larger than even Planos himself. His warriors marched in close order, each carrying a long pike and shield. They positioned themselves immediately behind Planos and Peter knew them to be Archon Plano's elite bodyguard.

Peter watched as the third troop of thousands of warriors ran out from the dust, screaming and charging forward in one great mass behind their leader who rode a black death horse. Peter recognized the leader to be the Archon Athemitos. His warriors were painted all blue from head to toe and wore heavy bearskins, and bear heads. They were a terrifying horde that showed no mercy and fought with a bloodlust that always struck fear in anyone they attacked. Since Krino had been defeated, they had raided all across the land. Now they had joined the army for one last battle. Peter grimaced at the sight of these warriors. He knew that they would willingly sacrifice themselves to take a walled city, using their bodies as ramps upon which others could climb over walls. He had seen them do it several times before.

Peter watched as the fourth troop of thousands of female warriors marched out of the dust led by a warrior woman, dressed in red body armor and riding a red death horse. She had long black hair and wore a black cape that fluttered in the wind behind her as she rode up to just beside Planos himself. Her warriors marched in tight order, all armored in red and carrying a shield and sword. They positioned themselves to one side of the bronze warriors. Peter had never seen these warriors before.

Finally, a troop of archers emerged out of the dust and behind them, great siege engines including catapults and siege towers. The archers ran forward to just behind the Kratos sentry line, and the siege engines rumbled into their positions between the different troops. Finally, after a full hour, the great army had positioned itself in front of the gates, and suddenly all became eerily silent. No sound emerged from either camp as the two armies looked at each other.

A command was given, and the Kratos knights suddenly turned their horses and rode off to one side of the army. Otherwise, the entire army stood silent.

Peter finally looked away and drank water from one of the barrels and glanced back over the tower to the rear gate. He saw the warriors packed below him in the river crossing itself behind the first gate. They would bear the brunt of the first attack and would be the first to die, he thought. But they had all volunteered and knew that their chances of survival were low. In fact, unless a miracle happened, all their chances of survival were low, he thought. He dismissed the thought and turned back to face the enemy. His army knew what to do, he thought. Now they would wait until Planos made the first move.

CHAPTER TWENTY EIGHT

A forest trail led through the valley of bones and Lillian ran to it as the three specters followed her. She heard Eleos fighting something back at the camp but could not reach him now. Her only way to escape was along the trail. The heavy fog gathered at her feet, covering the bones around her, breathing and pulsing the same way it had done when she first had entered the valley. She remembered what Eleos had told her about the fog.

"It only had control over you if you let it. Otherwise, it was harmless."

She ran through the fog, and it immediately retreated away from her, drawing back against the heavy brush to one side of the trail. She noticed with total amazement that as she ran past them, the bleached bones that lay all around her began to shake and move along the ground. She was too shocked to do anything but continue to run along the trail.

Lillian glanced back and saw that the three specters still chased her, their yellow eyes piercing, their shapes hidden by the flowing robes that covered their bodies. The trail curved toward the right and climbed a small hill to emerge in a large meadow that stretched far to the north to a mountain range covered in trees.

Lillian stopped at the edge of the meadow and stared across to the mountains. They were the same she had seen in Zanah's valley, but now she was on the same side of the cliffs, and only the meadow lay before her and the mountain range. The kingdom the Light had shown her before, even before Jonathan had found her, lay just beyond the meadow. But the meadow was too far across, and she could not keep running. She glanced back down the trail she had come but saw nothing but the thick brush. The trail no longer led back through the trees. Shapes moved through the brush, but she could not see what they were. What was she to do?

Lillian grabbed for the Light around her neck. In the Shadow Realm, the Light glowed and was warm to the touch, but here, in this realm, there was no Light around her neck, only a small jewel. The Light worked differently here, she thought. It seemed to be everywhere all at once, a part of the very environment she was in.

Lillian began to panic, not knowing which way to go or how she could reach the mountain range in time. Or what of Eleos? She thought. She looked around her but realized that she was totally lost. When the trail disappeared in the heavy brush, she now did not know how to find her way back to him. And what could she do, even if she did find him? She had no weapon, no way to defend herself when the specters that chased her emerged from the brush.

Her only chance was to run to the only hope that she had, the mountain range that offered security. Something screamed in the brush behind her, but she did not look back. She ran as fast as she could through the meadow covered in flowers. Her fear of what lay behind her overcame the peace offered by the meadow itself.

Meanwhile, Eleos gathered his thoughts and pulled himself back away from the body beside him. He recognized the laughter as coming from Zanah herself. That meant that the witch still had some control over Lillian or else she would never have been able to follow her through the portal to this realm. Now he knew what he had encountered. He had been fighting the deception in Lillian herself that she had yet to overcome. Even though she had been freed from the Shadow Realm, she had allowed Zanah somehow to still have some control over her.

Eleos watched as the body disappeared and he stood alone by the embers of the fire. He packed his gear into the small satchel he carried over his shoulder and retrieved his sword from where it lay by the fire and began walking in the last direction he had first seen the girl run the night before. The spell that had been cast over the girl had shielded his own sight, and he knew that she had been gone for at least an hour or more. But he also knew that she only had one way to go, and that was toward the mountain range to the north. The Kingdom pulled her toward it, even if she still did not fully realize what was happening.

He followed the trail through the brush among the bleached bones and saw that they had moved, gathering themselves together into piles along the trail. They continued to quiver and move as he passed and Eleos smiled to himself. Only Elohim could cause that to happen, which meant that the girl was closer to the Truth then she realized.

Eleos began to jog with a renewed assurance now that he fully understood who it was that he was dealing with. After a short time, he emerged from the brush into the meadow fully aglow in the sun's light, the distant Kingdom mountains sparkling like a jeweled necklace. The sight never ceased to amaze him, even after an eternity of witnessing its beauty and power.

Surely Lillian would be overcome with the meadow's peaceful power, yet he saw nothing of her at first and then, he sighted the girl, far off in the distance, running toward the mountain range. What was she running from? He thought. And then he saw three dark figures running close behind her, their evil presence wilting the flowers and lush grass as they passed, turning the beautiful vegetation into a swath of death and blackness.

"Psuche!" Eleos called, in his own language, "Lillian!" he shouted again, but the girl was too far from his voice to hear him, or she was too overcome by the deception.

Eleos sprinted across the meadow, trying desperately to catch up with the fleeing girl. If only she would stop and realize the salvation that lay all around her, he thought. But she still had lingering doubts about her worthiness, of the purity of her creation. The Shadow Realm still haunted her with past mistakes, failures, and unbelief. But Eleos could catch her. He was gaining ground as he ran through the blackened meadow, which was restored to its former beauty as he passed. His job was to impart Mercy at all cost.

Suddenly the dark specters turned to face him, their great broadswords dripping black oil over the flowers and immediately turning them to dust. Eleos drew his own sword and accepted their challenge for battle gladly. He rushed at the first one, ducking under the broadsword's downward swing, slicing through the specter's midsection that disappeared as the blade cut it in half.

Lillian looked behind her and realized that the specters had turned away from her, the heroic Eleos charging them with his upraised sword in hand. She looked around her, panting heavily. The mountain range was no closer than it had been before and all around where she stood, the meadow had turned into a black wasteland, dripping in oil and smelling of death. She had no weapon, but she would not let Elcos fight by himself. He risked his life for her, she thought. She had to help him!

Eleos turned to face the second specter, parrying its sword thrust and then he sidestepped and slashed at the third one and ducked back as the massive broadsword swept over his head. Wherever the specters stood, the meadow turned black, but wherever Eleos moved over the wasteland, the flowers immediately returned to their former glory.

Lillian saw a chance to assist when one of the specters backed toward her, but just as she moved forward, she heard a horn calling from somewhere over the meadow, a horn that she had heard many a time before in the Shadow Realm. The death horn of the Sahat. But how could that be? She was no longer in the Shadow Realm, she thought with confusion.

She turned again to face the sound, fear of a past life returning, and saw a dozen warriors, riding the black death horses, charging, the battle axes high over their heads. As they charged across the meadow, the flowers died and turned black. And for the first time, she no longer feared them. The thought of the warriors turning her beautiful garden into a wasteland infuriated her, and she knew that she would no longer run, but would stand her ground among the flowers that turned alive again as she walked among them. The same as she had seen happen as Eleos fought behind her.

The horsemen screamed at her, but she held her ground. The mighty horses rushed among her suddenly, but she held her ground with even more determination. They would not destroy her garden anymore, she declared!

And suddenly among the rush of horses and through the dust of battle, Lillian saw a warrior suddenly jump among the horses, slashing with a mighty sword. Horses screamed as they fell, throwing their riders across the meadow. Brilliant flashes of pure white light flared. All around her, the warriors fought, but she could not tell who was struggling to protect her. And then for a moment, she saw Jonathan fighting beside her, but there was someone else fighting among the multicolored rainbow as well. All around her the blackness of the meadow was replaced by the beautiful colorful flowers.

And then Lillian heard a voice call to her from beyond the mountains, it seemed, "Lillian."

The battle raged around her, but she seemed not to be standing anymore among the participants. All around her, shadows fought, but all she could hear was the voice of a woman calling to her.

"Lillian child, come to me. Come to me, and I will save you from the horrors around you."

Suddenly Lillian gasped in horror. The entire meadow was black and covered with the corpses of her family. Her father and mother, her cousins and childhood friends, all lay across the battlefield. Warriors fought as shadows around her, but she could hear nothing, and could only barely make out the forms as they fought.

And then she saw the most beautiful woman she had ever seen standing across the meadow from her, dressed in a royal gown, her hair adorned with jewels, her face glowing with beauty. Lillian took a step toward the woman, and suddenly the woman stood before her, looking down at her with bright, green eyes.

The woman caressed her cheek, lovingly, seductively and lowered her head and kissed her.

"Lillian, come back with me to the garden. You must be tired from your journey. You cannot keep fighting these shadows that haunt you. Come with me, and I will give you peace that you have been searching for," the woman spoke softly.

Lillian wanted to respond to her, to kiss her back and go with her, but instinctively, she reached for the Light around her neck, because deep within her, she knew that something was not right. She felt Jonathan's presence strong within herself, even though she had seen him fighting among the shadows.

The Light was only a jewel in this meadow. But when she touched it, the entire meadow suddenly glowed a brilliant white, causing the flowers to respond with a rainbow of bright colors that shot across the sky. The colors seemed to fill the universe and then she saw a man standing in the light behind the woman, the same man she had first seen long ago when Jonathan had first tried to save her from the attack by the river. The man smiled at her, and she suddenly knew exactly who he was. He was The Light, the Lamb of God.

Lillian looked back at the woman and immediately recognized who the woman was. She was Zanah.

Lillian stepped back and glared defiantly at the woman standing before her. Zanah suddenly looked confused and fearful as she realized that her power had been broken.

"I've had about enough of you, witch!" Lillian screamed and pulled the jewel from her neck. "You wanted me to give you the

Light. Well, you can have it," she stated defiantly and shoved the rock through the woman's throat.

Zanah backed away in horror and clasped the necklace, pulling the rock back out of the wound and blood gushed forward. For a moment, she thought that she had the Light itself, but then quickly realized that she only held the jewel in her hand. She turned, frantic, and faced the man standing in brilliant light behind her and with a realization of who it was who stood behind her, she screamed.

And suddenly the light vanished, taking Zanah with it. And it was all quiet again, and the meadow returned to normal.

Jonathan stood to one side with his back to her. A strange man stood nearby as well, dressed as Eleos and resembling him as if they were brothers. Her heart pounded with excitement and love. Once again, her soul mate and lover stood before her. Since she had fallen through the tunnels and landed in this strange land, she had felt his presence in a way that she could not truly understand. The emptiness that had been within her had filled beyond comprehension, and although he had not been with her on this journey, she knew somehow that he had never left her.

"Jonathan!" she exclaimed.

Jonathan turned to her, and she rushed to him as the strange man smiled widely. She jumped up in his arms as he caught her, hugging him tightly. Jonathan kissed her again and again.

"Oh, I missed you. I didn't know what to do. I thought at first that I had lost you again, but it seemed you were always here. And then Eleos found me. He saved my life, Jonathan."

Jonathan placed her back on her feet and looked over at Eleos, who walked up beside them, "Thank you Eleos, for what you have done to assist us."

Then Jonathan turned to Crestos, who stood behind him, "Lillian, this is Crestos."

Crestos bowed before the girl, taking her hand and gently kissing it. Lillian remembered him from when she had first fallen through the tunnels and blushed when he kissed her hand. Radiating from his presence was pure goodness and peace.

"I know him, Jonathan. He pulled me from the tunnel." she curtsied before him, smiling.

Crestos turned to face Eleos, "My dear brother, it is good to see you again."

"And you too, brother."

Lillian looked around her then. The meadow was as she had first seen it before running from the brush, "What has happened? Who were those monsters?" she asked.

"Let overs from the Shadow Realm, Lillian," Eleos answered. "You brought them with you when you crossed over, but I am very proud of you, mistress. You have overcome them."

"But I don't understand. In the Shadow Realm, the voice kept telling me that the true Kingdom was out here. That the garden I was in was only an illusion. Are we now in the true Kingdom?" Lillian asked.

Jonathan stood beside her and took her hand, "The Light told me the same thing. Where are we? And what of our friends back in the Shadow Realm? We have to return to help them."

Both men smiled, and Crestos answered, "You are in the very edge of the True Kingdom, but you are in the Shadow Realm as well."

"How can that be?" Jonathan asked.

Eleos continued, "Humans are incredibly complex beings. The Shadow Realm is full of mysteries, but you must remember, it was created in the image of the Creator. It was meant to be three in one, just as the Creator is three in one. But because of the curse, humanity became fragmented. All must be restored as it was meant to be. But even before then, when you are in the Shadow Realm, you can still be in the Kingdom as well."

Both Jonathan and Lillian still did not understand fully.

Crestos smiled, "Remember, you only see a portion now. When all is restored, you will see all. But now you are right. It is time for you to go back into the Shadow Realm. It is there that you all will finally see the true Kingdom for what it was meant to be."

Crestos pointed to the mountains. Follow the path in front of you, and you will find the Shadow Realm just over the ridge. Jonathan took Lillian's hand in his, and they turned toward the path.

MACKENZIE'S JOURNAL
DAY SIXTEEN

What must it have been like to walk in the garden in the cool of the day with God…..like Adam did…..

The same thing can happen now. Nothing in my creation has changed. I am still here. My greatest love, mankind, is still here. The garden is still present. But your perspective must change. You live in the physical creation where I have placed you. But your spirit can even now live in the spiritual garden where I first placed man.

You see the Tree of Life.

Forester, you understand trees. You work among them, see their beauty, understand their power. They are the greatest of the plant community I have created. They provide shelter, food, homes, and shade from the scorching sun. You walk among them, and they are real.

Change your perspective. The garden is presently a spiritual existence in this realm you call time. One day, I will totally melt the two together because I am a consuming fire. But now you live in both the physical and spiritual creation. Those who have awakened to my presence, who have embraced my son, who allows the Holy Spirit to inhabit the temple of God are a new creation. Old things have passed away. New things begin.

So, you walk even now in the forests of my garden. A garden I created for my love, my bride. For You.

Reach inside yourself. Look through the planes of existence through spiritual eyes, through my eyes that are now yours. Because as my son Jesus prayed before the cross in the garden, he prayed that you and I would be one as he and I are one.

So, look through my eyes, my sight, my spirit and you can see the Tree of Life. It stands tall, majestic, beautiful and strong, timeless. It shelters, protects, offers peace and shade. Its fruit is for the healing of the nations, for eternal life. You have gained access to the cross which is the true Tree of life.

I love to walk in the cool of the morning with each of you, my beloved bride. Because of the cross, you and I can become one again.

Walk with me in the garden each and every day. Talk with me. Express to me your deepest thoughts, your dreams, your fears, your sadness, your joy. Because they are also mine.

When you are afraid my child, run to me, and I will spread my wings of protection over you. When you are happy, dance with me under the stars of heaven among the lilies in the garden meadows. When you are tired, rest in the shade of the forest next to the stream of life that flows from my garden. When you are hungry, let us have a picnic among the grassy knolls together.

See the world around you now. There are countless children who live outside of my garden. The flashing sword still bars them from the Tree of Life. Not because I keep them from entering my rest, but because they don't know, don't understand, are afraid of the flaming sword.

I whisper to their spirit, shout from the mountain tops for them to enter in, but you need to provide the bridge. You are the gate to heaven. I will open, you, a window and pour out my spirit, my blessing on all mankind.

In your physical world when you find a beautiful place to visit, you tell everyone to come and experience what you have experienced.

So do the same in the spiritual world as well. Build bridges with people in the physical. Meet them where they are, see them for what I have created them to be and then build a relationship with them. Then I can flow through your gate and bring them into my garden as well.

One day all will be melted together, and we will live forever in unity in the garden that is even now all around you. Now bring my world into yours, heaven to earth, my kingdom into the world's kingdom.

But even as you do this, remember that anytime you wish, you can walk with me, hand in hand, in my garden that I have created just for you.

THE PHYSICAL REALITY

The girl placed the book on the table next to the bible after reading it three times through. She had never read such words of love. Never in her life had she ever heard of a God as loving as the one portrayed within the words. Her father had been a minister that had abused her while preaching of a God who poured out His wrath on anyone who disobeyed His law. At a young age, she had prayed the prayers. She had cried out to God for Him to love her, to forgive her of her sins. But she had never felt worthy because of the teachings of her father. Time after time as she grew into her early teens, she would come forward to an altar and pray to a God out of fear, always wishing for more, but always told that she was never good enough, that only Hell awaited her because of her sin.

And then one night her father came into her room while she slept and what he did to her caused more shame then she could bear. The next day she tried to kill herself, but her father found her in time, the knife by the bed, her blood soaking the sheets. She was sent to a church hospital by a father who was ashamed of her, and no one seemed to listen to her when she tried to explain her actions. He was a great man of God, they would say. A great evangelist, others would tell her. One nurse even suggested that it was her fault, that in her father's weakness, she had taken advantage of him, that he could never have done such a thing on purpose. But the girl knew better.

They told her that she needed to pray more for God to cleanse her of her sins. But she had tired of praying. The next day, she broke out of a window at night and ran away.

For a while she hitchhiked the state of Tennessee until she found a home among a group who lived in the remote mountains of North Carolina, traveling across the National Forest, but even that went wrong. Too many drugs and she found herself in the wrong place at the wrong time, and she had been attacked and left for dead. And then she had found herself in the home of this elderly woman in a place where she was surrounded by pure love and peace that she had never felt before.

As a young girl, she had prayed and felt the love that the book revealed, but that had been over ten years ago. What a peaceful place to be, she thought. And she drifted to sleep, dreaming of meadows covered in flowers and of a man standing by the trees, holding his arms to welcome her home.

CHAPTER TWENTY NINE

The gates of Soteria held strong as the mighty catapults heaved flaming balls of fire and huge boulders against them with incredible force. Occasionally, a missile would arch over the wall and fall harmlessly in the river, but most of the projectiles continued to pound at the gate, but after an hour, the gate still held.

Peter and Heather watched from the tower that rose high above the gate itself. The ground shook with each impact. Great clouds of smoke and dust rose upward. As fires spread and began to burn sections of the great gate, Peter ordered the men to pore water over the gate from a series of sprinklers that they had constructed, using water pumped upward to the tower from the great river itself.

Below the tower and behind the gate, the forward ranks of the Soterian army waited to defend the crossing when the gate finally did fall. And across the river, the great army waited quietly, just outside of the archer's range. Archon Planos had set himself up a table on a small rise behind the army, and through the telescope, Heather watched as he ate lunch as if nothing at all was happening.

"He's eating lunch," she commented incredulously.

"What?" Pete looked down to her.

"Planos is eating lunch, Peter."

Peter took the telescope and looked for himself and chuckled, giving the device back to Heather. He shook his head but said nothing as he watched another stone crash against the base of the gate. This one broke through in one small place. A few more direct hits at that spot and a gap would be opened, he thought.

The warriors behind the gate saw the opening from their side as well, and immediately great timbers were brought forward, and repairs were made to try and close the gap. Another boulder crashed into the opening and broke through, knocking the warriors back and killing or wounding several. More timbers were quickly brought forward, and the opening was reinforced just in time as a third rock hit the same spot. Whoever was manning that particular catapult was very good, Peter thought.

Peter signaled his own catapult that sat back on a small hill across the river using the flags. Soon a ball of fire arched over his head and fell harmlessly across the river in front of the first rank of warriors. Peter signaled the catapult again and a second fireball arched through the sky. However, this one landed a few feet in front of one of the catapults across the river, scattering the warriors positioned in front of it. A third missile arched overhead and hit the catapult directly, obliterating it and a great shout arose from the Soterian ranks as they watched the siege engine collapse.

Peter saw the commander of the enemy artillery rush forward and suddenly the rocks flew over the gates in a blind attempt to hit the catapult that had destroyed one of their own, but they could not see the Soterian catapult because of the great wall along the river. The repair teams had enough time to strengthen the gate somewhat, but not enough. Sooner or later the gate would collapse and then the army would rush forward.

When Archon Planos saw one of his own siege engines suddenly explode in a great ball of fire, he stood from his table after taking one last gulp of wine and mounted his horse. He galloped across the battlefield to where Archon Athemitos stood with his barbaric horde and then rode to the artillery commander. Peter watched as the men talked and then Archon Planos rode back to his bodyguard. Great horns blared from across the plains, and the horde army screamed a bloodthirsty shout and suddenly rushed forward as the siege engines hurled flaming missiles against the towers that stood on either side of the gate. One shattered against the base of the tower, knocking Heather down as fire swept upward suddenly. Peter rushed to spray water, but the pumps had been destroyed.

The bell towers rang and archers flooded the air with flaming missiles over the tower walls. Other archers stood in the towers themselves and shot down upon the sudden rush of horde warriors. More Soterian warriors climbed the tower steps to man the walls, but another missile crashed into the base and destroyed the steps, killing many who were trying to climb them.

Peter shouted to Nathan below and ordered his troop to retreat to the second gate if the towers fell and then rushed back to the front of the wall to look down among the carnage below. As he expected, the horde warriors, driven by a demonic, bloodlust that did not fear death, began swarming up the sides of the tower walls, piling their own dead to build a ramp of horde flesh which soon would allow them access to the tower itself.

Enemy archers suddenly ran forward and began to add their own missiles to the larger fireballs that pelted the towers and front gate as the fires quickly spread. Heather grabbed a dead archer's longbow and began firing down into the growing army below. Young Carmen stood beside her, bravely throwing oil-covered rocks downward that spread fire over the horde warriors.

It had happened so quickly, Peter thought. They were holding out, and just a minute later the towers were being overrun with warriors who would quickly gain access to the top and could then cross the bridges over the river to the other side. Peter had given orders to destroy the bridges and retreat, but the army was coming forward too quickly.

Peter rushed over to the tower bell, where the nervous sentry from the night before now lay wounded and bleeding severely on the floor. He rang the bell for retreat and pulled the injured sentry back from the wall.

"Heather!" he screamed, but she did not hear him.

"Heather, we have to leave!" he ordered, and this time the girl turned.

Peter saw the banners fall from the other tower and knew that they had fallen and suddenly there was a great explosion, and the other bridge fell into the river. Peter grabbed at several archers, screaming at them to retreat across the river. One pulled at the sentry and dragged him behind him as he ran to safety.

Suddenly a dark form jumped from behind the fires and Heather screamed as she thrust her sword at the figure. Several other warriors climbed over the dead and gained access to the tower, pulling down the banners to let the army below know that they too had gained access to the tower. Carmen fought bravely among the warriors, but he was too small, and they were too many. Peter lunged forward, killing one and knocking the second back over the wall, grabbing for Carmen and throwing him back away from the burning wall.

"Run, Carmen! You have to set the charges!" Peter screamed at the young man

Carmen stood for a moment and then acknowledged the order and ran back across the bride, terribly wounded and bleeding.

Peter then grabbed at Heather and pulled her from the struggle, killing the closest warrior with one great slash with his broadsword.

"Heather, you have to go!" he screamed and then seeing that she would not leave, he looked directly into her eyes.

"Heather, please you have to go, Help the wounded get across the bridge. I will be across shortly," he spoke calmly, assuring her, but she knew that he most likely would not make it across the bridge. He kissed her forehead and turned toward the onrushing warriors.

Heather rushed back across the bridge, crying as she ran. Carmen had fallen before her, gravely wounded and she stopped to pull him across, but he appeared to be dead. She pulled him across the bridge anyway and laid him within the second tower where warriors stood ready to defend it. Below her, the second gate was closing as the ground troops retreated.

Peter stood alone in the tower as Kratos warriors suddenly climbed over the wall to face him. He knew the first one.

"Well, well I see we have the traitor cornered," the knight said and rushed forward.

Peter parried the blow and sidestepped, slashing low and hard at the warrior, the blade severing the leg, and the man fell screaming in pain. Two more jumped over the wall, and Peter turned to face them, but suddenly, the Soterian knight, Nathan, jumped forward and killed one instantly and knocked the second one back over the wall.

"Nathan! I ordered you back" Peter shouted.

"And let you have all the glory Peter," Nathan smiled as more Kratos knights appeared over the wall in greater numbers than before.

At the second tower, Carmen suddenly came to and grabbed for Heather.

"Heather, we have to blow up the bridge."

Heather looked across the bridge and saw both Peter and Nathan fighting dozens of enemy warriors. She would not leave them there to die.

"No! I won't leave them there!" she screamed.

Peter pulled at Nathan, "We have to get across the bridge. They will blow the bridge, Nathan!"

Nathan turned away, and they both began to run back across the bridge, but a lance thrust suddenly forward toward Peter, and Nathan sidestepped quickly and took the full force of the thrust that was meant for Peter. He fell against Peter and Peter turned fast to catch him.

"Nathan!"

Peter held him up, the lance impaled through the man's side. They were in the middle of the bridge now just above the charges. The enemy rushed forward, but because of the width of the bridge, there was room for only two abreast.

"Go, Peter, I know my destiny!" Nathan shouted and suddenly lunged forward toward the approaching enemy, brandishing his great broadsword over his head, screaming, "For the Light and the Truth!"

He drove the enemy back, throwing several over the bridge before he too fell, carrying several with him down into the mighty river. The enemy warriors crashed into seething waters, screaming as the strange silver phantoms pulled them under the mighty current. But Nathan fell silently and disappeared into the river to re-immerge further down where the current was slow and peaceful where villagers pulled his body from the water.

Peter turned and ran as Carmen set the charge, and the bridge exploded behind him as he fell within the second tower. Now only the second bridge and two guard towers stood before the great army.

Heather hugged Peter, and he noticed that she was wounded and had been burned by the fire. The wounded sentry lay to one side, now dead as was the young Carmen, who had carried out Peter's orders just before he had collapsed.

Peter pulled Heather away from him and looked at the men and women who stood in the tower. Many of them were wounded. He had to let the past few moments remain in the past. Now he had to lead the army forward.

He looked over the battlefield across the river. The two towers were burning as was the gate. Soon the enemy would be able to cross the river. They could bring their catapults forward and begin pounding the second gate. It was only a matter of time before they would gain access to the second gate as well and then Soteria would fall. Jonathan had said to hold the crossing at all cost. He was their only hope now. Peter did not understand what was happening, but he knew that all he had to do was hold out until Jonathan and Lillian came back, and the Apostolos Or would save them. He grabbed the Light around his neck and felt reassured that in the end, all would be fine.

"Heather, help the wounded back to the village, and you go with them," Peter ordered.

"I won't leave you, Peter," she stated.

"Please, Heather. You are wounded. Take care of yourself and then return, but please get the wounded help."

She turned and began to help the others down the steps to the villagers below. The meadow was already full of wounded men and women. It had happened so quickly, she thought.

CHAPTER THIRTY

Jonathan and Lillian took one step down the path and immediately stood on the ridge, looking down into a great valley below. Jonathan gasped.

"What is it?" Lillian asked.

"I have been here before," Jonathan stated.

A great valley spread out before them, covered in great forests and interspersed with lush meadows. To one side, a great waterfall cascaded down over a cliff to fall into a deep pool. Back against the meadows, a village stood peacefully, the many homes scattered all through the trees. Beautiful gardens, well tended and full of vegetables and fruits grew throughout the village.

Lillian gasped in astonishment as well, " Jonathan. I have seen this place. This is the village that I saw through the fog, the place the voice told me was the kingdom. The place the voice said was virtue, peace, and joy. We have made it!"

Jonathan stepped forward. He could not believe his eyes. He stood in the valley that he knew to be the village of Soteria. How could this be the kingdom?

"Lillian. This can't be the kingdom. I have been here before. This is Soteria. This is the village across the great river where the fugitives have been fleeing to since the Light set us free."

How could this be?

Lillian turned to look back from where they had just come from. Far behind them lay the vast meadow full of flowers that blew in the wind. Far below them, she could see both Crestos and Eleos standing among the flowers.

"No, Jonathan. We are in the kingdom. Look."

Jonathan turned and saw the meadow behind him as well, and he remembered the first time he had seen the valley. It was when he had first seen the fourth man in the fire, the slain lamb on the mountain. He had seen himself disappear and the great valley below him beneath the blood-stained cross. This was the Kingdom of God. Soteria had been the Kingdom of God all along. The

Shadow Realm was disappearing, yet Soteria appeared to not have changed at all.

And then Jonathan knew without any doubt at all that they were standing in the Garden of God, the Kingdom. The Garden of God had been all around him the entire time that he had been in Soteria, but he did not know it. Crestos had said that even while they were in the Shadow Realm, they could also be in the garden. It took the Shadow Realm itself to disappear before the Kingdom to fully become a reality.

And then Jonathan thought of the servant girl Gloria. She had said that she was the Shadow Realm and that to save her, he would have to unite with Lillian. It was all beginning to make sense now, he thought. Humankind was created in the image of their Creator, to be three in one just as the Creator is three in one. Body, soul, and spirit. He and Lillian were only two of the three. They now had to save the third one for all to be redeemed, but how?

And then Jonathan saw black smoke rising above the forest on the horizon in the direction that he knew lay the river crossing.

"Lillian, remember the servant girl, Gloria?" Jonathan asked.

"Yes. What happened to her?"

"I'm not sure, but I think she is near. See the smoke. This place is under attack. We have to hurry before it is too late."

They both ran down the trail to the village, which was empty and continued through the village to the forest on the other side. A path led by the stone tower at the village gate and toward the river crossing and they took it. They continued to run toward the smoke until they suddenly stopped on a small rise overlooking the river. Below them lay an encampment full of warriors, men, women, and children. Great fires were burning across the river and to one side lay hundreds of dead and dying people. Women walked among the wounded, handing out food and drink and applying bandages. The great towers and gate that blocked the river crossing were under siege by a great army across the river.

To Jonathan's relief, the gates were still holding, and the river crossing had not been taken, but at what cost? Lillian took his hand as they walked down toward the people and as they recognized him, they stopped what they were doing and bowed in respect. The Apostolos Or had returned. The two of three had been reunited, and total redemption was near. People begin to run across the army, and the word spread quickly.

A few moments later, Heather heard the call that Jonathan had returned from where she lay under a tree, too wounded to return to Peter who stood guard in the tower. Her wounds were too great, the burns to severe and she could no longer fight. She forced herself up as Jonathan and Lillian walked toward her. The two looked glorious, she thought.

Jonathan noticed and ran to her, kneeling next to her as she collapsed back down on her back.

She smiled."I knew you would return. We have held just as you said. Jonathan."

Jonathan held her hand in his as Lillian knelt beside them.

"You have done great, Heather. Don't worry. Our time is almost upon us, and all will be restored." he comforted her, his heart breaking because of the suffering that she had endured. She had been the first one that he had brought the Light to, the first one that had been saved from the chains of death. Even though, severely wounded, her spirit was strong.

Heather looked over at Lillian, "So this is your true love, Jonathan."

Jonathan blushed, "Yes this is my Lillian. Lillian, this is Heather."

Lillian took Heather's hand in hers. "It is so good to meet you. Jonathan has told me much about you."

Heather smiled, "Oh trust me. He has told us everything about you. You are so beautiful, all that he described. And now you are united."

Suddenly Peter rushed forward and stopped, shocked at the sight of Heather and then grabbed Jonathan as he stood up and embraced him.

"You have returned, Jonathan."

"Yes, I have returned, and I wish for you to meet Lillian." Jonathan stepped back and helped Lillian to her feet.

"So, this is your true love, Jonathan," he stated as Heather laughed.

Jonathan blushed again, "Yes my friend, this is my true love and our salvation as well."

Lillian bowed as Peter took her hand in his and kissed it lightly, bowing to her as well, "My Lady. I'm so glad to finally meet you in person."

Peter stood back suddenly at attention, "Jonathan we lost the far side of the river yesterday, but so far the wall on this side has held, although we have lost one of the towers. I don't know how long we can hold before they break through. Most of the army is either dead or wounded," he sighed.

"I'm sorry, Jonathan. So many have given their lives."

Jonathan took Peter by the hand, "Don't worry, dear friend. You have done well. I never could have led the army in battle the way you have. But our time is near. I know now what Lillian and I have to do. I have seen much the last few months, and I know that the truth of the Light is about to be fully revealed."

Jonathan smiled and looked at Lillian who knew what he was thinking, because they were truly united, two of the three. Only one more to go.

"And I want everyone to witness our salvation. Peter you don't have to fight anymore. No one does. Gather the villagers. Have everyone throw down their weapons and take off their armor. Bring everyone to the river, all the wounded, even all of the dead. Lay the dead by the river and the wounded under the fruit trees and place the ones who can stand in a line where all can see." Jonathan ordered.

Peter looked incredulously at Jonathan because of the order.

"It's okay, Peter. Do what I say. All will be revealed, and I want all to be there when it happens."

Jonathan took Lillian by the hand and walked up to the gate that stood at the river crossing. He heard the crashing of the missiles as they struck the other side, but the gate was strong and held. The two stood behind the gate silently, hand in hand, two of the three untied entirely, waiting now for the third to finally arrive. They could feel her presence somewhere on the other side of the gate. They could also feel the strong presence of the Light itself on the other side of the gate as well.

A few minutes later, Peter walked up beside Jonathan, carrying Heather in his arms. He was dressed in soft leather pants and loosed fitting shirt, she in a white dress, flowers in her hair. Jonathan recognized the dress as the same one given to her by the Light when her chains had been removed on the first night by the monuments after the attack of the nomad camp. Peter placed her beside him, where she leaned against him for balance and strength.

Jonathan turned to her and leaned down and kissed her softly on the cheek.

"You look as beautiful as that first night when the Light freed you of the chains of death," he said, even though the side of her face was blistered because of her burns.

All around them, the villagers of Soteria gathered, helping the wounded and laying the dead along the river shore. Jonathan waited until all of the villagers arrived as the missiles kept hitting the far side of the gate in front of them. He thought of all that had happened. Of the first night in the cave of his fears when he had first seen Gloria and had first retrieved the Light. She had said that he had saved her, but in a way, she had saved them all, because she had the Light herself before it had been stripped from her by the Sahat. He thought of Captain Patrick, who had taught him how to use the sword and who had said that he, long ago could have been the Apostolos Or, but had turned from the Light. He thought of how he had come upon the nomad camp and had met Lillian, of how he had crossed over to Soteria and defeated Krino and had won the freedom to all in the Shadow Realm. These actions had led to the Shadow Realm crumbling and the true Kingdom being revealed. Now there were two of three, and the third was approaching. He braced himself and took Lillian by the hand and ordered the gates to be open.

CHAPTER THIRTY ONE

The gates swung open outward and a missile flew through the open gate and landed harmlessly behind the villagers. A great horn blew across the river, and the artillery ceased firing. Jonathan and Lillian walked out into the river crossing and was astonished at the carnage across the river. Thousands of warriors lay dead all along the banks of the river. Fires burned along the plains, and the Shadow Realm continued to diminish, crumbling to the very riverbanks in places. Suddenly the gates and tower behind them crumbled as well, and Lillian glanced behind her as the rocks vanished and only the forest and meadows remained. The villagers stood silently all along the riverbanks. The two walked out into the middle of the river and stopped, and suddenly all was deathly still.

The warriors that were left in Archon Planos' army formed ranks along the far side of the river, and Archon Planos himself rode out to the very edge of the river and stopped just short of the water.

"So, the great and mighty Apostolos Or himself and his harlot have arrived. You are too late to save your precious Shadow Realm. In fact, you have stupidly left the safety of your once great wall and have foolishly entered my realm once more. When I am through with you, I will destroy Soteria as well." Planos challenged.

Jonathan said nothing. He and Lillian both now knew exactly what they needed to do.

Planos laughed and shouted back to the warriors behind him, "Bring the servant girl forward."

The ranks parted, and Gloria was brought forward naked and in chains. She looked the same as when he had first seen her in the cave so long ago. He held Lillian's hand tighter and forced himself to look at the girl as she stood before him, but this time there was no fear in her eyes. She smiled at him and stared straight ahead.

"I was told that you could have saved this girl before in the cave, but you were a pathetic fugitive then," Planos shouted.

"That was a long time ago Planos. Much has changed since then." Jonathan responded.

Planos laughed, "Yes it has, but that does not matter. The law requires that mankind must pay for his sins. You are only two, and I have the third. Without all three, you will be nothing, and I will have won. Where is your Creator now? God has left you to die here on the river."

"If we are to die, then at least let us die together, Planos," Jonathan challenged.

Planos thought for a moment and then laughed, "Oh, you try to trick me. No. You will die together, that I am certain, but on my terms, not yours," and he waved his arm.

Suddenly the ground shook all around them, and Jonathan and Lillian held each other closer to prevent them both from falling off the crossing and into the river's current, but the Light within them flooded them with peace, and they knew what was to happen and was not afraid. Their goal was to be reunited with the Shadow Realm that now, was only the servant girl, Gloria.

A great dark cloud rose from the ground and engulfed Planos, and he disappeared within its blackness. A shape began to take form in the gloom and fire erupted outward from the blackness, and suddenly the black cloud vanished, and a great, red dragon stood on the shore by the river. The villagers across the river gasped in fear at the great monster before them, but they stood bravely and watched. Both Jonathan and Lillian was taken by surprise by the sight and did not have time to react to the soldiers who suddenly charged them, placed chains around them and led them to the shore.

The dragon laughed, "I am the great one, the shining star, the great Lucifer. You wanted to die together, well now you get your chance," and he waved his arm.

The soldiers took the three and placed them on a cross that had been placed at the river, tying each of them to the cross beams by ropes so that they all three hung beside each other.

The dragon re challenged the three, "Where is your God now? Where is the Lamb you say was slain? The fourth man in the fire? The Light of the world? Elohim? The Bene Elohim? They have all forsaken you."

Suddenly a voice called from the mountains that all could hear.

"MAY YOUR WHOLE SPIRIT, SOUL, AND BODY BE KEPT BLAMELESS AT THE COMING OF OUR LORD, JESUS"

And the dragon suddenly backed away and looked upward toward the heavens. A great white light shot forward, and a man materialized out of the light and stood at the river crossing.

The three hung on the cross and looked down at the man that stood below them and immediately recognized him. They had seen Him many times. First, He had appeared as the fourth man in the fire when the fugitives had been attacked by the Sahat while they had hidden in a tree on the Plains of Apistia. Then He had appeared in the Light when they had met Him by the wagons on the night when the nomads had been attacked. He had shown Himself again to them on the mountaintop when they had first seen the slain Lamb of God. He had waved his hand and destroyed the Sahat by the monuments when Heather had been rescued. He had appeared before them when Patrick had finally reached Soteria, gravely wounded. They realized that he had always been with them throughout their journey. In their world, he was known as Elohim, but he was also Bene Elohim, the Son of God. But now they knew his name to be Jesus.

Jesus looked into the three's eyes and they felt a peace that transcended all understanding. He said nothing to them but smiled knowingly and walked across the river crossing to where the dragon stood.

The dragon hissed and stepped back against the cliff wall that stood immediately next to the river itself. He had nowhere to retreat to, because the entire Shadow Realm had disappeared, leaving only the three hanging on the cross, and the soldiers on one side of the river and the Soterians on the other side.

"The Shadow Realm belongs to me," the dragon challenged, "By Elohim's own command, the Shadow Realm must die for its rebellion."

Jesus shook His head in agreement, "Yes you are correct, the Shadow Realm must die. But I will make a trade."

The dragon lowered his head in thought, "A trade?"

"Yes, Lucifer. I will give you myself for the Shadow Realm's life." Jesus answered quietly so that only the dragon could hear his words.

The dragon backed up in disbelief. Surely this was crazy. He thought. Why would the Son of God give his life for such as the Shadow Realm?

"Why would you do such a thing? Humanity rejected you. Humanity sinned against God. Humanity is not worthy of you. Even I know this to be so."

"Lucifer, the reason why is of no concern of yours. You don't have the ability any more to understand. You gave that right up when you, yourself rebelled against the Father. Now I offer a trade. I will die for them." Jesus answered.

The dragon laughed at the heavens at his good fortune, "So be it. If you wish to give your life for such as the Shadow Realm, then that is fine by me."

The dragon motioned for the soldiers to take Jesus and they hung him on a cross next to the three. The stupidity, Lucifer thought. Jesus would die next to the three who would die along side of him. The dragon did not understand that the three hanging on the cross with Jesus was exactly what Jesus had in mind to begin with.

When death came to Jesus, everyone heard him say, "It is finished."

The dragon laughed again and completely agreed with those words. The Shadow Realm was finally dead, he thought to himself. Soon Soteria would be destroyed as well.

Great storm clouds rolled in from the heavens and lightning crashed. The wind blew, and blackness settled over the land for three days as the dragon looked on amazed at what was happening.

The three looked on as they hung on the cross themselves and wondered at the great sight before them as all the wounded villagers suddenly were made whole and the dead ones stood up alive. Suddenly Patrick stood among them and Captain Connelly and all the dead nomads. One by one the villagers turned into some type of vapor and flew into the man who hung on the cross. The soldiers themselves, everyone that had been a part of the Shadow Realm turned into vapor and flew into the man on the cross. All did so until only Peter and Heather remained. The three watched as Peter and Heather embraced and then they too turned into vapor and disappeared into the cross and Jonathan knew that everyone, both good and bad were a part of the Shadow Realm and that Jesus, the Light of the World, on the cross was redeeming everything back to him.

And after three days, only the three remained by the river and the man on the cross lay dead at their feet and the dragon stood to one side, rejoicing at what he thought was his victory.

But on the third day, the man suddenly came alive, and the dragon screamed in pain and vanished, and only Soteria remained in all its' beauty and the three in one creation, the perfect humanity, stood in the Garden of God, with a risen Savior, and all was redeemed to what it was meant to be.

CHAPTER THIRTY TWO

I stood in the middle of the Garden of God, body, soul and spirit, all united as was the perfect will of God from the time God first breathed His life into my being. You have known me as the Shadow Realm throughout the discourse of this story, but I stand here a new creation.

For as far as the eye could see, a wondrous garden spread outward toward the far mountain cliffs, sparkling with multicolored jewels. Deep blue water cascaded down across the face of the cliffs, the bright sunlight shining through and creating brilliant rainbows of promise.

Closer in, a meadow covered in flowers and scattered, majestic trees blanketed the landscape. A river meandered through the meadow; the banks lined with trees that bore fruit in all seasons. Brilliant shafts of white light shone through the forest from a distant source and I followed the shafts of light with my gaze until I saw the source of the light which was a gate constructed within the canyon walls. The gate stood open revealing a city sparkling brightly among the rainbow.

I turned and saw immediately beside me, the Risen Savior, Jesus. He smiled at me and immediately, I remembered from before when He had first created me and breathed life into my being.

And then I saw two separate scenes through what appeared to be windows to other worlds. One was a kitchen where I sat crying with an elderly woman. And the second, my entire story from the cave of my fears to the cross by the river. So much pain, fear, death, and disbelief.

I stood for a moment confused by the sight before me, especially when the entire story rewound backwards to the very point when I had first found the Light and then collapsed entirely into the man hanging on a cross.

And then suddenly, I understood completely. I looked again to Jesus and he smiled widely and shook his head in agreement with my sudden revelation. The Lamb of God was slain for my sins before the world was even created. Which meant that all had already been redeemed back to God before my story even began. The Shadow Realm was only an illusion created by the fall of man, but it was not the truth from the very beginning. The true reality was the garden where I now stood. From the time I had first found the Light, I had been in the garden all along.

"The Shadow Realm is only true if mankind does not accept the gift I have given. You are a new creation, an eternal being whose rightful place is in my garden even while you live in the earthly realm." Jesus said.

And I looked more intently into the only window left, the one where I sat at the kitchen table.

THE PHYSICAL REALITY

Gloria woke from the best sleep she had ever remembered, the words of the book still fresh in her mind. A warm sun shone through the window and washed over her young face, and her stomach stirred from the sweet smell of bacon cooking in the kitchen. She stretched and taking the book, she walked into the kitchen. Nicole turned to her and smiled, and she sat down at the table.

"Good morning, child. Sleep well?" Nicole asked as she placed the food on the table and sat across from the girl. Nicole had prayed for the girl for most of the night, knowing in her heart that God had brought the girl to her in this place and this time for her to finally understand the true Father's love.

"Yes, I did. Thank you for what you have given me. I had no place to go and here, I feel.....peace."

"No problem child. You can stay for as long as you need to," Nicole said and looked at the book for the first time.

"You read Tom's journal?" Nicole asked.

"Yes. I hope you didn't mind. I found it last night before I went to sleep. It is beautiful. I can't explain how it made me feel. Who wrote it?"

Nicole smiled and reached for the book, taking it in her hands and caressed the cover and placed it back on the table, "My husband, long ago."

"Where did he find the words? I never knew that God could be as the book portrayed."

Nicole smiled, "Tom always loved to write. We were very young then and was trying to raise a family," Nicole stood up and retrieved a picture and set it on the table, "Here he is and our three children."

The picture was of Tom and Nicole and three children, the oldest not more than ten. Gloria took the picture and looked at the young family. They seemed so happy.

Nicole continued, "We were youth ministers then, but it was a bad time as well. I was very sick, and Tom tried so hard to take care of us, but we never seemed to have enough. He wrote this after an accident where he almost died. He was a wildland firefighter and was on a fire in Wyoming when he had been trapped by the fire. He was never the same when he returned. Before, he had been depressed, on the point of death and hopelessness. He had even tried to kill himself. But after the accident, he was changed, a new man. He wrote this soon afterward and printed one copy, the copy you have now. I have kept it ever since."

"Where is he now?" Gloria asked.

"Oh child, he died a few years ago."

"I'm sorry," Gloria said softly, regretting such a dumb question.

"Oh, it is okay. All is well. He is in heaven now, and I will soon go to join him. We raised three beautiful children and have six grandchildren and fourteen great-grandchildren. They are all coming soon for my birthday, I would love for you to meet them."

Gloria smiled, "That would be nice."

Gloria looked down at the book. She desperately wanted to know more. She wanted to feel the peace that seemed to be all over the woman who set before her. Nicole knew, through the Holy Spirit, that the girl wished to come home to the Father's loving embrace.

"Child, what is it that you really want to know?" Nicole asked.

And Gloria began to cry. A few hours later, after a long session of the young girl telling all and Nicole sharing a Father's true love with her, a new creation was born, and all was redeemed back to what God had originally intended for her to be. From her mother's womb, the Father knew Gloria by name. God created Gloria in her mother's womb and wrote the poem that is her life before she breathed her first breathe in this world. She was created a threefold being, body, soul and spirit. However before, in the expanse of eternity, the Father already knew her. He already made a way for her redemption. When He had first created her, He had placed her in His garden. Now she had finally returned. And it was as if she had never left Him.

AFTERWARDS (Long Before)

There is only one time since light began that darkness has ruled. In the infancy of this world, before the creation of the garden, a way had to be made for you to walk hand in hand with me once again. The matter was settled, my bride secured, redeemed even before the betrayal.

I died; you know. At the point of my death, all of creation stood still because the source of all creation lay separated entirely in death. For a moment light no longer existed except within me who was dead.

Mankind witnessed this moment and made an accurate account of it but did not understand the true significance of what they saw. My body laid dead, a lamb sacrificed before the creation of the world, and terrible blackness settled over the hill where I died for just a moment.

Do you know that at that moment when darkness settled over me, time stopped in your world, terrifying blackness covered the entire world all at once, not just at Golgotha, but across every mountain, every valley, to the furthest reaches of the universe.

All became trapped within the blackness of death. For just a moment that could have been an eternity.

The enemy loves darkness, gains strength from its coldness, boldness from fear. They swarmed through the depths of the heavens, driving straight for me as I lay in death, thinking that in my death, they ruled.

My servants froze, not from fear, but from trust in their creator.

Some say that I risked too much. What if death won? What if the sacrifice was in vain?

I was not worried.

In that moment of my death, when all of creation was covered in the horror of total separation, when time stood still, and the universe froze in total silence, only one sound could be heard.

I screamed in total anguish, pain, fear, horror, desperation. A scream that echoed through the ages, a cry that pulled all of the life from me as I took all of mankind's death into me.

And then a challenge of victory and light exploded forward from all that I am, and the enemy that drove toward me screamed in horror as the light engulfed them, and my servants fell upon them, and my enemy was driven to the ground in final defeat.

And light burst forward in your soul and you became a new creation in me, and you gained access back into the garden that I created just for you, my bride. All you must do is say yes to my marriage proposal.

IT IS FINISHED..

Most of the character names as well as the place names found in the Shadow Realm and Mackenzie's Journal come from the Greek and Hebrew and have very interesting meanings. If one took the time to look up the meanings of these words, one could peel back a layer from the text and may find deeper revelations, or maybe not? I thought about adding a dictionary here, but what would be the fun of that? A good source to learn more about what the names mean would be Vine's Complete Expository Dictionary of Old and New Testament Words by W. E Vine, Merrill F. Unger and William White. Jr.

If the reader wishes to know more about Tom and Nicole Mackenzie, then I suggest reading my novel titled, Gatekeepers Journey Mackenzie's Revenant, that reveals more interesting realms that run through and over the Shadow Realm across the very expanse of time itself.

Also Tom and Nicole Mackenzie's journeys through the realms continues in my novel titled, Garden House.

And keep a look out for future stories as the different realms around us open and close and reveal worlds that lay just beyond our reach, just out of sight, but always present. Tom and Nicole found a few in their lifetime. Hopefully one day I can tell more of their story.

Jody Brady

JUSTICE PROJECT

The Justice Project is an outreach ministry of Unified City Church whose main purpose is to be the hand of God to the world. We look for the darkest reaches of humanity and then plant the Light of the Kingdom of God in the middle of it.
We strive to constantly think of ways to assist people in need, to share the love of Christ though a helping hand in times of crisis. We look past the shape of humanity and see God's greatest creation through the eyes of Christ. We see the destiny within all of God's children, not the current circumstances, but God's reality. We wish to help people in a time of need and then walk with them as they journey toward God's destiny for them.

We wish to fulfill the words of Isaiah 58.
- Loose the chains of injustice
- Set the oppressed free
- Share food with the hungry
- Provide shelter
- Clothe the world
- Untie the cords of the yoke of bondage

For more information about our many ongoing projects and how you can help us be the Hands of God to a hurting world, email us at justiceproject@unifiedcitychurch.com.

Made in the USA
Columbia, SC
23 September 2024